He's real good-lookin', isn't he?

Pam could've sworn she heard the words through her stethoscope as she examined Angie.

He thinks you're pretty, too.

Maybe she'd been working too hard. Hallucinations *were* a sign of stress. She cleared her throat. "Uh, Mr. O'Toole, would you step outside a moment?" She exited the cubicle, Mr. O'Toole close on her heels. Too close, she thought. She could actually feel his gaze on the back of her neck.

"Is she all right?" he asked. "She gave me some crazy story about being an angel and how she gets to pick her parents." One side of his lips hitched up in a half smile. "Conjures up interesting possibilities, though, doesn't it?"

"Mr. O'Toole, I don't even know you—nor do I like you!"

He came within inches of her and looked down at her suggestively. "Then how come your pulse is beating like crazy?"

Dear Reader,

Christmas might be meant for kids, but I'm still a great believer in Santa Claus. Here are a few things I've asked him to deliver to your house this year:

A stocking stuffed with caring friends to make the good days memorable, and the bad days bearable;

A box filled with laughter that you can unwrap and enjoy whenever you feel the need;

Garlands of hope, because without a keen sense of optimism the future looks bleaker than it really is;

A bright package full of opportunities to help someone else, the surest way to lift your own spirits and bring a smile to your heart;

A sprinkling of wisdom to help you keep your life in balance and your priorities straight;

The knowledge that just by being you, you're a valuable person. I know you are to me.

Have a very Merry Christmas and the happiest of New Years.

Sincerely,

Charlotte Maclay

P.S. I love to hear from my readers. Write me at: P.O. Box 505, Torrance, CA 90508.

CHARLOTTE MACLAY
THE LITTLEST ANGEL

Harlequin Books

TORONTO • NEW YORK • LONDON
AMSTERDAM • PARIS • SYDNEY • HAMBURG
STOCKHOLM • ATHENS • TOKYO • MILAN
MADRID • WARSAW • BUDAPEST • AUCKLAND

ISBN 0-373-16657-5

THE LITTLEST ANGEL

Copyright © 1996 by Charlotte Lobb.

Prologue

"It appears there has been a mistake."

Saint Peter's voice rumbled in his chest, but it didn't scare Angelica Rhoades, even if she was only six years old. He had a nice lap to sit on and he smelled good, too. His long, white beard was real soft when it brushed against her cheek.

"You mean my name's not written down in your book?"

He turned one page after another. "This volume only goes until the year 2050. That would imply you should have had a long life."

"But I didn't."

"Yes, as I say, an error has been made. A serious error. We don't usually do that."

"Are you gonna fix it?" People had to fix things when they messed up. Angie had already learned that. Probably because she'd messed up so often in her life. Like the time she'd broken her foster mother's fancy hand mirror, one that was real, real old. Angie had tried extra hard to glue it back together again but she couldn't make it look quite right. A week later the so-cial worker had taken her to another foster home. She hadn't stayed there long, either.

"You could remain here with us, if you'd like."

This seemed like a nice enough place. There was a big, fancy gate made out of gold and there were fluffy clouds to walk on. Somebody was playing pretty music nearby and singing nice songs. Certainly it was better than the last foster home she'd lived in. There'd been mice that made noises in the walls at night and there hadn't been much food to eat. And it had been cold. Real cold. She supposed it was the furnace that had started the fire. Or maybe one of the other kids had been playing with matches. She'd never do that.

"Or you could return to earth, if you would prefer," he suggested, "and live out the remainder of your nat-ural life."

"Until my name comes up in the book?"

"That's right."

She frowned. "Would I get to pick my own parents this time?"

"That could be arranged, I suppose. Given the un-usual circumstances."

"I wouldn't want to be poor no more."

"Poor isn't necessarily bad."

"Rich would be better." Concentrating hard on her decision, she peered over the edge of the clouds. It was a long way back down to earth, but she'd mostly liked it there—the green grass and pretty trees with branches that blew back and forth in the wind. For some reason, plain old white clouds didn't seem all that interesting. And it didn't look like there were many toys here. Not that she'd hardly ever owned a toy of her own. Least ways, not brand-new ones. "I don't want to be cold, either, or sick all the time like I was before."

"I can understand that."

"Could I have a horse?"

He closed his eyes and sighed. "You should not ask for too much Angelica. It's called greed, one of the world's greatest sins."

"Didn't do no harm to ask." She lifted her shoulders in a shrug and grinned at Saint Peter. "Okay, I'll go back down there."

"Very well, if that's your choice. But there is one other thing you should know."

"What's that?"

"You'll only have a few weeks in which to find your new parents. If you don't, or if the people you choose don't want you, you'll have to come back and we'll make adjustments in the book." His eyes were a soft blue like the sky was on a summer day and he looked a little sad, as if he doubted anybody would really want her. "You see, God likes to have all of his littlest angels in heaven to help Him celebrate Christmas."

Chapter One

An old guy with a long, white beard waved him off the freeway onto a detour. P. T. "Lucky" O'Toole figured the highway department must have a special program to hire senior citizens because the man looked to be at least a hundred years old.

Following instructions, Lucky downshifted and whipped his Italian sports car onto the main street of Meadowbrook, an inland town that lay halfway between Los Angeles and San Diego. Though his horse-breeding farm was only a few miles away, he rarely passed through the small community. There were far quicker routes to the Del Mar racetrack on the coast.

Silver garlands decorated the light poles along the street, each one topped off by a big red bow. Store windows sported bright paintings of snowmen, elves and Santa Clauses. Kinda cute and folksy, he thought. Hometown, U.S.A.

Another guy, who looked to be the bearded twin of the first highway worker, held up a detour sign, signaling Lucky to make a left turn. Caught off guard by the sudden ordered change in direction, he downshifted again and cranked the wheel hard.

The car went into a slide. It shouldn't have. He had the vehicle completely under control. He hadn't been speeding. Much. The noonday sun was bright and the street as dry as a bone.

He reversed the wheel, turning it into the skid, and tapped the brakes. It didn't help. The car kept traveling sideways toward a life-size nativity scene on the front lawn of the big stone church at the corner.

His eyes widened. All the figures placed in and around the display were made of plaster. Except the angel perched on top of the makeshift wooden stable. She was a real-life kid dressed in white, a lopsided halo cocked at an impish angle over her forehead. She grinned mischievously, like an unrepentant little devil, and winked.

"No! Get out of the way. Jump!" His warning did no good. She just sat there as if she'd been waiting all day for him to show up.

Though the nuns at Saint Michael's Orphanage had taught him well, O'Toole didn't often pray anymore. But in that instant before he collided with the crèche, he closed his eyes, braced himself for the impact, and sent up a heartfelt plea. "Please God, don't let me kill the kid."

PAMELA JONES—Dr. Pam, as her pint-size patients called her—hurried across the street from the Inland Pediatric Clinic toward the emergency entrance of

Meadowbrook Community Hospital. She'd hoped to enjoy a quiet lunch hour between patient appointments, but apparently that wasn't to be. An understaffed hospital and an accident somewhere in town had conspired against her, according to the urgent phone call from the emergency room supervising nurse.

As so often happened when she approached this particular entrance to the hospital, a shiver of apprehension sped down her spine. She'd come here that night three years ago when her husband Ted had died. He'd been dead on arrival, though they hadn't told her that on the phone—an automobile accident, a speeding drunk driver behind the wheel of the other car.

The entire hospital staff and many of the townspeople had grieved the loss of the founder of the Inland Pediatric Clinic, but none more so than she. There was still a hollow place in her chest that used to be filled by his love. She tried valiantly to make her medical practice at the clinic substitute for what had been so violently torn from her life. It didn't always work.

She strode past a parked ambulance and went in through the emergency entrance.

"Dr. Pam, I'm really sorry I had to call you," said the supervising nurse, Irene McDonald. "Dr. Khaja is tied up in surgery, and I thought someone should look at the little girl they brought in a few minutes ago. A traffic accident. I think she may have a concussion."

"It's all right, Irene. Eating lunch is probably a bad habit anyway."

"Ah, if that's what keeps you so slim, how come it doesn't work for me?" The nurse patted her large, very pregnant abdomen.

"Guess from now on you'll have to stay away from those watermelon seeds—and Ralph," Pam teased. The expected wash of pain that she had never carried a child close to her heart came and went quickly this time. She had a patient to see. "Where's the girl?"

With a friendly smile, Irene directed her to cubicle three.

The emergency room was set up in a semicircular layout, with medical beds partitioned by floor-to-ceiling drapes on one side and the medical station on the other, where nurses and emergency technicians could keep an eye on all the patients at once. Pam retrieved her stethoscope from the pocket of her smock and headed for bay three. Anxiety, or maybe it was a lingering sense of loss, continued to edge along her spine.

From within the cubicle she heard the contagious sound of childish giggles and she pulled back the curtain. Suddenly her steps faltered.

No one had warned her there was a man waiting with the injured child, a man with a devastatingly attractive smile that creased both of his cheeks and lit up his blue eyes as if he were right on the verge of laughing out loud. Something about that smile gave Pam an uncharacteristic desire to laugh with him, and she flushed at the prospect.

O'TOOLE HAD NEVER before known what it meant to be poleaxed. It was like getting punched in the gut by a world-class boxer. The doctor walked into the cubicle and he figured he might never breathe again. He had a trained eye for thoroughbreds. He could spot classic lines at the distance of a furlong and appreciated smooth flanks from any angle. Full across the chest was good, too. She qualified in all respects, running away from the field.

Her chestnut hair shone like it had been recently brushed, and it rested in a softening curve against a determined jaw. Her nose was straight, eyes intelligent, and her lips looked as if they had been designed for kissing.

No woman, and sure as hell not an M.D., had a right to look that good in beige slacks and a shapeless lab coat. Even so, his entire body responded in a way so powerful it almost drove him to his knees.

It had to be lust, he decided. Too long without a woman. Any other reason would have sent him sprinting from the emergency room as fast as his legs would carry him.

No way could his reaction have anything to do with what the kid on the gurney had been telling him.

All business, the doctor barely spared him a glance before she switched her attention to her patient.

"Hello there, young lady," she said with the hint of a smile. "What's your name?"

"She's Angelica Rhoades," O'Toole said. "But she likes to be called Angie." The doctor looked at him and he nearly sank into her soft, brown eyes—eyes that should belong to every kid's mother and every man's lover.

"You're her father?"

"Me? No." He quickly denied the possibility. "I'm O'Toole. My friends call me Lucky. I'm the guy who hit her."

A double row of frown lines creased her forehead. "You hit her?"

"My car went out of control. It shouldn't have. It just skidded for no reason at all. Right into the nativity scene where Angie was sitting up on top. Fortunately, I don't think she's hurt real bad." Though she'd sure been saying some crazy things, O'Toole admitted to himself.

"Were you injured, too?" She looked at him as though she suspected he had experienced serious brain damage.

"Not a scratch. Though the crèche didn't do as well. I'm going to owe big-time on that."

The doctor cocked her head. Kinda cute the way she did that, he thought. Made her look young. A little vulnerable.

"Have you been drinking, Mr. O'Toole?"

"Nah, not me. You want to see my AA card?"

She didn't laugh at his little joke. "Have her parents been notified?"

"I don't exactly think so."

"Where are your parents?" she asked the child.

"I don't have any," Angie said, glancing from O'Toole to Dr. Pam and back again. She smiled a devilish little grin that made her blue eyes light up with a wicked spark of mischief. "Least ways, I don't have any *yet.*"

"Then do you live with someone else? Maybe an aunt or uncle?" Pam leaned over the child, using her flashlight to check the relative dilation of her pupils. Both were even and responsive.

"No, ma'am."

"Where do you live?"

"I've lived a whole bunch of places."

"Here in Meadowbrook?"

"I don't think so. Unless it was when I was just a kid."

Pam suppressed a smile. Angie looked to be no more than six and had a good many years left to still be a kid, though there was a hint of something ageless in her eyes. From the lack of body fat, Pam surmised she was slightly undernourished, with a possible history of chronic illness. Her wispy blond hair looked as if someone had taken pinking sheers to it, and none too skillfully.

Pam switched to the stethoscope, which she warmed first with her palm. A strong, healthy heart beat rapidly in the child's chest, probably a little accelerated from the excitement of the accident and ambulance ride.

"Take a deep breath for me, honey." Pam listened to the chest sounds while wondering about the man standing on the opposite side of the gurney. He seemed too big, too tall, too vibrantly alive to fit within the close confines of this small cubicle. Except for a few squint lines and the faint shadow of whiskers, his face was unmarked, as though in his thirty-some years he'd had no cares in the world. A perpetual smile teased at the corners of his full lips and danced in his bright sapphire eyes. Unruly dark hair feathered his shirt collar, the hint of a cleft softened his otherwise square jaw. From the cut of his shirt and faded jeans, she guessed he was a wanna-be California cowboy down on his luck.

The fact that he was a stranger, not the child's father, however, made his concern and presence both touching and oddly appealing.

Not that she had any special interest in Mr. O'Toole. None at all. There was simply no reason she should give in to the urge to test the silky texture of his unmanageable hair with her fingertips. She had no idea where that thought had even come from.

He's real good-lookin', isn't he?

The childish words of admiration startled Pam. She could have sworn she'd heard them through her stethoscope, not as though they'd actually been spoken aloud. Her gaze darted to Angie's face. "What?"

He thinks you're pretty, too.

Pam nearly lost her balance. She grabbed the bed's guardrail to steady herself. Maybe she'd been working too hard. Hallucinations—and hearing voices—were definitely a sign of stress. She didn't at all like the sense of being out of control.

She cleared her throat. "Mr. O'Toole, would you step outside with me for a moment?"

"Sure, Doc." One side of his lips hitched up a little higher, threatening a full-blown smile. "I think there are a lot of things we need to talk about."

His tone, with its definite sexual innuendo, sent something warm and quite unexpected curling through her midsection.

Lifting her chin, she sent him a quelling look that normally put a halt to any undue familiarity. It didn't budge this guy. To her dismay, she felt a blush creeping up her neck. She hadn't done that since med school when the male students had been commenting rather explicitly on the feminine attributes of a cadaver.

She turned to the child. "You wait right here, Angie. I'll get back to you in a minute."

"It's okay. You and Lucky go ahead and talk. You need to get to know each other."

Pam blinked. Though the child didn't have any signs of a concussion, she was certainly acting peculiar. The odd comments, or what Pam thought she had heard, simply didn't fit. The absence of memory regarding her home and family were troubling, too.

She exited the curtained cubicle, acutely aware of Mr. O'Toole close on her heels. Too close, she suspected. She could all but feel the heat of his gaze on the back of her neck as she marched resolutely across the room to the nurses' station.

"Is she all right?" O'Toole asked.

"I can't find anything physically wrong with her that a couple of good meals wouldn't fix."

"Whew, that's a relief."

He jammed his hands into the pockets of his well-worn jeans, causing the faded denim to tug across his hips and drawing Pam's attention in the process. She had the distinct impression he was very well endowed.

Her gaze snapped up. She wasn't the sort who had that kind of a thought. Ever.

"See, the fact is," he continued in a lazy drawl, "since the accident, she's been talking kinda funny."

"Oh? How's that?"

"She's been giving me some crazy story about how she died years before she should have, and now she gets to pick her own parents."

"Oh, dear. That is troubling." Pam picked up the child's chart and noted some comments. That simple action gave her an excuse not to look into Mr. O'Toole's amazingly blue eyes—Irish eyes that kept on smiling and making her feel oddly uncomfortable. "I'll have to get the hospital social worker down here to talk to Angie about her parents. I may have to arrange a pediatric psych referral, too."

"She doesn't exactly seem *crazy* crazy. Just a little confused."

"Any accident can be disorienting for a child."

"I figured that." He leaned an elbow on the counter. "But you ought to know, the parents she says she's picked out are you and me."

Her jaw went slack. "I beg your pardon?"

His grin widened. "The idea conjures up a whole raft of interesting possibilities, doesn't it?"

She bristled. "It certainly does not."

"How come? Are you married? I don't see a ring."

"Widowed."

"My condolences. How 'bout kids?"

"No. Not that it's any concern of yours, Mr. O'Toole."

"Call me Lucky. All my friends do."

"I'm not your friend, *Mister* O'Toole. I'm Angie's physician."

He lifted a single, well-formed brow. "I gather you don't like me, Doc."

"I neither like nor dislike you, *Mister* O'Toole. My only concern is for my patient."

"Then how come your pulse is beating like crazy?"

Instinctively, she clamped her hand across her left carotid artery, the spot where her blood was pounding so heavily she could barely hear his words. How could he know? How could he possibly tell, when she'd only barely been aware of her own riotous reaction to how close he was standing? To the words he'd said?

Grinning, he told her, "I have that effect on a lot of women."

"I am not a lot of women." She turned and dropped the chart back onto the nurses' desk.

"Yeah, you're definitely special."

His intimately personal baritone voice slicked over her nerve endings like a hot flame, melting her insides.

"What makes you think you'd be such a wonderful father for Angie?" she asked, her voice suddenly more high-pitched than she would have liked.

"Hey, it wasn't my idea."

"What do you do for a living, Mr. O'Toole?"

He simply grinned at her refusal to use his nickname. "Guess you could say I play the horses."

Her eyes widened. "You're a gambler?"

"Some would say that. Got my start at a track in the Midwest when I was about fifteen. I picked up a winning two-dollar ticket that somebody had tossed aside. Parlayed that into seven winners, claimed a horse in a stakes race, and since then, everybody's called me Lucky."

"I don't believe in luck, Mr. O'Toole." She delivered her most steely look. "I believe in hard work."

"It figures. I suppose that means you're going to tell Angie that today was her raunchy-luck day. No parents available in this town. Try someplace else."

"My job is to contact the social worker. She'll take care of—"

"Is that how you'd like your own kid treated?"

"I told you, I don't have any children." Though she and her husband Ted had certainly exerted a good deal of effort during the last three years of their marriage, after she had completed her residency, to get her pregnant. Sadly, it hadn't worked. And then it had been too late. He was gone, and she was left with the knowledge that she had been inadequate as a woman.

"You should be a mom. You've got real nice eyes."

To Pam's surprise, a band tightened around her chest, and she felt the press of tears. "I believe this conversation is becoming far too personal."

"I suppose you're right." He ran his fingers through his hair. The gesture did little to alter the uncombed effect of his dark, thick waves.

To Pam's horror and complete fascination, he then had the audacity to tuck a strand of her hair back behind her ear. A river of gooseflesh sped from the point he had touched to somewhere warm and achy in her midsection.

"But it's kinda too bad you don't believe in luck—like me running into Angie and her looking for a mom and dad. We'd make a helluva pair, wouldn't we?"

"I think not, Mr. O'Toole." She swallowed hard. "Definitely not."

Turning abruptly, she left O'Toole standing there contemplating her response while she went in search of a little privacy and a phone to call the social worker.

He drummed his fingers on the counter, amazed at how the faint scent of roses lingered after the doc had walked away. Her perfume did a darn good job of making him forget he was in a hospital, where medicinal smells should have overwhelmed his senses. Instead he was thinking about the softness of rose petals and how the doc's skin would feel just as good.

He'd gotten himself into a real fix this time. He didn't want Angie to end up in an orphanage. His childhood experiences had soured him on that option for any youngster. But he wasn't all that confident of his own parental abilities, and he wasn't sure he could change the doc's mind about a collaboration. Achieving that goal would be a long shot, at best, and maybe not necessarily a wise move for either of them.

He smiled to himself. It'd be a helluva lot of fun to try, though. A challenge like gaining the trust of a spirited horse. Success could mean a big reward.

ANGIE LOOKED UP at the ceiling above her hospital bed in the emergency room. Every square had a bunch of holes in it. She was a good counter and liked numbers real well, but every time she got up to twenty or so, she lost track of where she was and had to start all over again.

She wished Lucky and Dr. Pam would finish getting to know each other. She didn't much like being in a hospital. It smelled funny. She was ready to go home anytime they were.

"Angelica." Saint Peter's voice seemed to come out of the holes in the ceiling like it was a great big stereo set. "Are you positive these are the two people who you want to be your parents?"

"Sure. They're both real nice."

"I agree. But I had assumed you would select a married couple. Perhaps a family with children who would be your brothers and sisters."

"I don't want no brothers and sisters." She puffed out her lower lip. "I picked Dr. Pam and Lucky."

"They are not at all suited to each other."

"Then you gotta help 'em get suited."

"I have been helping. But in issues of the heart, things are not necessarily easy."

"It don't matter. You promised."

"Indeed, I did." Saint Peter sighed deeply, fluttering the curtains that surrounded Angie's bed. "You have made matters very difficult for me."

"I'm gonna be real good so they'll wanna keep me."

"Yes, I know you'll try."

"So can I go home now? To my new house?" Where Angie just happened to know there were horses. She'd seen 'em from up there in the clouds but hadn't told Saint Peter. That would be her little secret.

"You will have to be patient, Angelica. This is going to be far more complicated than I had anticipated."

Chapter Two

"They've even tried checking with the police," Pam said.

Since giving Angie a thorough exam and contacting the social worker, she'd gone back to the clinic and seen six patients—two runny noses, an ear infection, a suspected case of chicken pox that turned out to be an early onset of acne, a broken arm, and a child complaining of recurrent stomach aches, which probably meant he didn't want to go to school. Returning to the emergency room, she discovered the hospital social worker had made no progress at all in locating Angie's family.

And that Lucky O'Toole was still practically camped at Angie's bedside. Or hovering next to the nurses' station.

"She's not a criminal," he said, his beautifully arched eyebrows lowering into a frown.

"That's not what I meant. I thought perhaps her parents or a guardian would have filed a missing person's report by now."

"You don't believe her story about picking us out as her parents?"

"Hardly." Impossible, as far as Pam was concerned. "Maybe she's a runaway."

"Six is a little young for that, don't you think?"

"I don't know. My younger brother Reggie took off on his tricycle when he was three years old. An hour later, after frantically searching the neighborhood, my folks found him two miles from home pedaling as fast as his little legs would go." Pam smiled at the memory. In some ways, at age nineteen, Reggie was still trying to run away, at least from becoming a grown-up. But then, her father had always had the same problem of not taking his responsibilities seriously.

"I waited till I was fourteen to take off," O'Toole commented in a casual tone, as if all children left home sooner or later. "But nobody came after me."

Pam shot him a glance. She didn't want to feel sorry for a man who'd run away and felt no one had cared. "Please, Mr. O'Toole, this is a hospital matter we're talking about. Perhaps you could wait in the lobby?" Or at the closest racetrack, if he'd prefer. Putting him at the greatest distance possible would be her choice.

"Angie wants me to stick around."

Pam didn't. He made her decidedly uncomfortable. His interest in her was a little too keen, and she didn't want to resume the discussion of the two of them becoming parents of anyone, including Angelica Rhoades. "Until I can get matters straightened out, Angie will simply have to remain in limbo here at the hospital."

"She isn't going to like that."

"What can I do? The social worker tried to call Children's Services and there wasn't even an answer."

"They're still out to lunch?"

"Shouldn't be. Not at this hour. Maybe it's a county holiday and nobody told us," Pam grumbled. "Or the circuits are overloaded." She really wanted to get this matter settled. That appeared to be the only way she'd get rid of O'Toole. "I also checked and found there are no listings in any telephone book in the entire county for a Rhoades. Which seems a little strange in and of itself, since that isn't a particularly unusual name. It's like someone scooped up all the telephone books and erased that particular name. It's odd, really," she mused.

"So what are you going to do with her?" O'Toole asked.

"I suppose I could take her to the county home myself, but I'm reluctant to do that without being able to confirm with Children's Services first. Sometimes they don't have any empty beds."

"No!" O'Toole protested vehemently. "You can't put her in an orphanage."

"It would only be a temporary measure until we can locate her parents."

"I don't think she has any."

Pam gaped at him. "You don't really believe her story about wanting us . . . you and me . . . I mean, that she thinks we should be her . . ."

"Parents." O'Toole filled in the blank. "Yeah, I think I do."

The curtain swung open on Angie's cubicle. "I gotta go pee," she announced. The hem of her full-size hospital gown dragged on the floor and the flap hung open down her back. The outfit made Pam think of a tiny cartoon ghost who needed a big hug.

"Okay, kid." O'Toole extended his hand. "I'll show you where."

"Now wait a minute." Pam grabbed his arm before he linked up with the child. His biceps was rock solid, and she felt a current of pure, electric heat warming her fingers through the fabric of his shirt. She pulled her hand away as if she'd been burned.

"What is it?" he asked.

She resisted checking her fingertips to see if they had been singed. "You're a nonrelative male. No way am I going to let you take a six-year-old girl to the rest room on your own. In fact, you shouldn't even be here in the emergency room with her."

He cocked her an indolent smile. "If that's the way you want it, Doc, you can take her."

"I will." She reached for the child and tiny fingers closed tightly around her hand. A band echoed the same feeling around her heart.

As they passed the desk where Irene was checking charts, the nurse whispered sotto voce, "Wow, is he a hunk, or what? If I didn't already have Ralph housebroken, I'd latch on to him."

Pam ignored the comment. She didn't need a man in her life who played the horses. She already had an irresponsible brother, a sister with two darling children who couldn't get her act together, aging parents and a pediatric clinic that was running several thousand dollars a month in the hole because of her policy to take every patient who came in the door—insured or not. She and Ted had decided that's the kind of clinic they wanted. The fact that he'd died hadn't changed her personal feelings about serving the community.

Sighing, she opened the rest room door. "Can you manage on your own, honey?"

"Maybe you oughta help. This gown thing is funny."

"Okay."

Under the gown the child was wearing simple white underpants that were gray from too many washings. Her legs were too thin for a six year old, her belly too flat.

In Pam's practice she saw a lot of children who suffered because of poverty and malnutrition. She couldn't take them all home to feed and fatten up. She'd been taught to remain objective. It wasn't always easy, particularly when O'Toole kept talking about parenthood.

Angie squirmed off the toilet seat and pulled up her pants. "Don't you like kids?"

"Of course I do. That's why I became a pediatrician."

"But don't you want one of your own?"

"I would have liked very much to have children of my own, but that doesn't seem possible. Besides, I'm not married."

"Lucky would marry you."

"Honey, I just met the man. I don't want to marry him." At the moment, he was at the bottom of a very short list that included absolutely no prospects. But that didn't make any difference. No matter how long the list, he'd still be right down there with the unemployed used-car salesman and the shyster lawyer she'd briefly dated since Ted's death.

"I'd be a real good little girl. If you have fancy mirrors and stuff, I'd be real careful not to break anything. Honest, I would."

Fighting tears, Pam broke her resolve to remain objective. She pulled the child into her arms. In spite of her ragged appearance, Angie smelled heavenly—sweet and clean and in need of a lot of loving. Maybe more love than Pam had left over after she took care of all her other responsibilities.

"Honey, everything will be all right. I promise." She should never make a promise to a child she couldn't guarantee. Pam knew that. Their health and happiness weren't entirely in her hands. But Angie, she sensed, needed to hear some words of hope. Or maybe, at this particular instant, Pam needed a little encouragement, too. Sometimes her responsibilities weighed too heavily on her shoulders, and this seemed to be one of those days.

She took Angie back to her bed, making a point to ignore O'Toole, then stopped at Irene's desk.

"I'm going to admit Angie as an in-patient," Pam said.

Irene looked up in surprise. "I thought she was all right."

"Let's just say my decision is medically justified on the basis she may have a concussion, and I need to have her observed for at least twenty-four hours."

"Meaning you don't want her to go to the county home. Assuming Martha Do-Good upstairs was even competent enough to contact them."

"Meaning her folks are bound to show up soon." How could any parents possibly stay away from a child as endearing as Angelica Rhoades?

"The hospital administrator isn't going to like this," Irene warned. "As far as we know, she's an indigent with no Medi-Cal card. Arnold, thrifty bean counter that he is, isn't going to want the hospital to foot the bill."

"I know. If he finds out, promise him I'll pay the overnight charges myself. I'm *not* going to throw her out in the cold."

"Atta girl!" Grinning, Irene gave her a thumbs-up. "You're all heart, Dr. Pam. No wonder all three of my kids love you."

SEVERAL HOURS AND a dozen patients later, Pam stepped out of the clinic, closed and locked the door, turned and almost ran right into Lucky O'Toole.

"What are you doing here?" she asked. His arms were filled with assorted stuffed animals, games and books, and a trio of colorful tethered balloons that stretched up into the night sky.

"I was gonna go see Angie. I thought you'd like to come along and then we can do dinner."

"What?"

"You haven't eaten, have you?"

"Well, no, but—"

"Great. You can check on your patient, then we'll—"

"The hospital would have called me if Angie needed any medical attention."

"Yeah, but—"

"O'Toole, you're being presumptuous. I have other plans for this evening." Like a hot bath and a good night's sleep.

"Like what? You got a date?"

"No," she admitted, then wished she hadn't. Thinking there was another man in her life might have gotten O'Toole out of her hair.

"So what's the big deal? You have to eat, don't you?" Somehow, in spite of all the goodies he was carrying, he managed to catch her arm and was escorting her toward the hospital.

"Not with you."

"With Angie then. We could order up from the hospital cafeteria."

"Obviously you've never eaten any of their food."

"Okay, then we'll have a pizza delivered."

"To a hospital?"

"Sure. Why not? It's not like we're going to feed junk food to all the patients on the floor."

"You're outrageous, O'Toole." The hospital doors automatically swung open in front of them.

"Yeah, I guess I am. You wanna be outrageous with me? I bet we could find some quiet, dark spot. Maybe the linen closet—"

"No. Definitely not." She choked down a laugh. "I have my image to maintain." Though the image that came to her was much more heated than her cool medical persona—sweaty bodies, arms and legs wrapped around each other, an impossible, improbable image.

"Darn. Guess if you won't go out to dinner, you're stuck playing gin rummy with Angie."

"She's only six. Wouldn't Go Fish be a little more age appropriate?"

"Hell, no. She's already into me for $2.57."

"You played her for real money?"

"She wanted a dollar a point. Luckily, I agreed to a penny instead, or she would have wiped me out. Watch her, Doc. She plays a mean game of cards."

The gray-haired volunteer at the information desk greeted Lucky warmly. Obviously, he'd already turned her into a fan.

Pam stepped into the elevator in front of him and smiled at the waiting passenger. "Hello, Mrs. Othello. How are you?"

The tall, angular woman smiled in response. "I'm about to be a grandma again. Number five. A boy, they tell me."

"Congratulations."

O'Toole pressed the button for the third floor where both obstetric and pediatric services were located.

"I imagine they'll call you to take a look at him when he finally arrives on the scene," Mrs. Othello said. "Shouldn't be much longer now. Poor Betsy's been here since six this morning."

"I'll be sure to check before I leave the hospital," Pam assured her.

"Wouldn't know what any of the grandkids would do without you, Dr. Pam."

"They're why I'm here."

The elevator doors slid open at the third floor. The expectant grandmother went left down the corridor. Pam and O'Toole walked in the opposite direction.

"Do you know everyone in town?" he asked falling into step beside her.

"If they are mothers or grandmothers, I probably do. Most of the pediatricians prefer to locate their practices in Escondido, where the big Tri-Cities Hospital is."

"But you prefer small towns."

"Ted—my husband—felt it was important that a small community have top notch service available close to home. I agreed."

"He didn't want any competition."

She snapped an angry look in O'Toole's direction. "My husband was an excellent medical practitioner. So am I."

"Yes, ma'am." He made a gesture of surrender that failed to erase the teasing glint from his eyes. "I have the utmost confidence in your talents, Dr. Pam. All of them."

A ridiculous, adolescent flush crept up Pam's neck as she walked into Angie's room. She had to stop reacting to O'Toole's double entendres like that. Unrepentant flirt that he was, she knew he didn't mean a word he said. And, at some very painful level, enjoying a round or two of bantering repartee with O'Toole made her feel disloyal to Ted's memory.

Angie was sitting cross-legged in the middle of her bed. Her eyes lit up at the load of toys O'Toole was carrying.

"Wow! Are those all for me?"

"Naw. I thought I'd give them to the kids down the hall."

Her face crumpled.

"He's teasing you, Angie." Pam's heart nearly broke at the child's dejected expression.

"It's okay," she said, hanging her head. "I didn't mean to be greedy."

If Pam had been standing a little closer to O'Toole, she would have given him a solid elbow to the ribs. She'd rarely seen a child more needy, a deprivation that appeared to go much deeper than simply a desire for a few toys. Emotionally, Angie couldn't handle O'Toole's jocular style.

"Hey, sport, don't look so glum." O'Toole sat down on the edge of the bed. "The doc's right. Everything I've got belongs to you." He shoved the teddy bear into her spindly arms and she hugged it tightly while he tied the balloons to her wrist. Her big blue eyes watched him intently.

"Is the bear really mine, enough so's I could give him a name?"

"Sure. Any name you want."

She scrunched her mouth sideways as she thought. "How 'bout Tony? I had a friend named Tony once. We were gonna be together forever and ever, but he got real sick and I didn't ever see him again."

"Tony, it is," O'Toole agreed. "Is he ticklish?" He threatened the bear's tummy with a twirling fingertip.

Angie giggled. "Teddy bears aren't ticklish!"

"Oh, no? How 'bout little girls?" He changed the angle of attack, causing the giggles to escalate when he made contact with Angie's tummy.

A lump formed in Pam's throat. Maybe a good dose of fun was exactly what Angie needed. Oddly, she wondered if she would benefit from the same sort of medicine, and quickly rejected the idea. She had a practice to run, a clinic in trouble, and her own family problems. There was no time for frivolous activities in her life.

"Do I gots to stay here much longer?" Angie asked when her laughter subsided.

"At least until tomorrow," Pam said. "By then, the social worker will have had a chance to make some sort of arrangements for you."

"I don't want any 'rangements." She puffed out her lower lip. "I wanna go home with you and Lucky."

"That's not possible, Angie. Mr. O'Toole and I don't live together."

"You could if you wanted," the child said stubbornly. "Lucky's got a real big house."

Pam's gaze met his across the bed and held for a heartbeat. Did he really want to take on the responsibility of a six-year-old child? Or was he thinking about playing house with Pam, not the youngster? A thought that was suddenly far too prominent in her own thinking. "Why don't we wait and see what happens tomorrow?" she hedged.

"Come on, you two gloom and doomers." O'Toole produced a childish board game with bright pictures and silly sayings from the heap of goodies he'd purchased. "They told me at the toy store any adult, with a modicum of intelligence, can beat a kid at this game. I figure that gives me an edge of eight-to-five with you, kid. How 'bout it?"

An hour and a half later, Angie had wiped out both Pam and O'Toole. Twice. Had they been playing for money, the Inland Pediatric Clinic's debt would have risen substantially. And Pam's ribs ached with laughter.

Instinctively, Pam leaned over to kiss Angie goodnight. "It's past your bedtime, sweet thing. Sleep tight."

Troubled blue eyes looked up at her. "I'll see you tomorrow?"

"I always check on my patients before I go to the office. I'll be here about the time you're eating breakfast."

O'Toole said his good-nights, too, and they left the room together.

"Hey, I forgot to order us up some pizza." He hooked his arm around her waist. "You must be starved. Guess we'll have to have dinner together after all."

She stepped away from the warm, enticing press of his palm. "Sorry. I have to check on the expected newborn."

"After that? I can wait."

"No. Thank you."

"I have the distinct impression you're trying to avoid me, Doc."

"You're a very clever man, Mr. O'Toole. I *am* trying to avoid you." Desperately. "Don't you have anything else to do with your time in lieu of pursuing me?"

"Nothing that can't wait."

Pam supposed a gambler would feel that way. Her father and brother had never felt any urgency about getting on with the serious business of life, either. Her sister wasn't much better. Perhaps that was why Ted, as a hardworking resident, had appealed to her so. She'd been confident their life together would provide the order and security she very much craved.

It hadn't exactly worked out as she had hoped.

LUCKY O'TOOLE stood in the middle of his living room. The housekeeper had been in that day. He could smell the lemon wax she'd used on the furniture and the clutter he usually left around the place had been put back in order.

He wasn't sure how Angie had known, but she'd been right. He did live in a big house. A mansion, by most people's standards. Even the nuns at Saint Michael's would have agreed he'd done all right since he ran away twenty years ago. And they would have been the last ones to expect Patrick Terence O'Toole—the runt of the playground and the clown in the classroom—to have succeeded.

But fifteen rooms, furnished lavishly by the most expensive home decorator he'd been able to hire, didn't make his house a home.

It was too quiet inside the sprawling two-story stucco structure. Too empty of life except when he threw his big Fourth of July party for horse trainers and owners, or had a few of the guys in for a game of cards.

No wonder he spent most of his time in the horse barns with old Rafael, his foreman, and the other workers who cared for his string of thoroughbreds. Lucky didn't much like being alone.

He marveled that he hadn't realized that before. He'd been so proud of all he'd accomplished—all that he'd acquired—he'd forgotten there was no one to share it with except Rafael. And his foreman didn't give a fig for original oil paintings or fancy brocaded upholstery.

Hell, neither did Lucky.

He tossed his jacket over the end of the banister and headed for the kitchen, flipping lights on as he went. Dr. Pam might not have been hungry, but he sure was.

In the refrigerator he found a beer, twisted off the cap, and took a long swig. The tangy coolness slid down his throat. He found the cooked roast his housekeeper had left for him and hauled it out to put on the counter. With a deftness born of experience, he lathered a couple of slices of white bread with mayonnaise and made himself a sandwich.

The whole idea of him being a father was ludicrous when he stopped to think about it. Mostly, he didn't want Angie, or any kid, to be stuck in an orphanage or shuttled between foster homes. That kind of life was no fun at all.

Now, the idea of shacking up with the doc was a whole different matter. He could handle that. Not that she seemed exactly interested.

He grinned. The way she blushed suggested she didn't have all that much experience with men, even if she had been married. Of course, under normal circumstances, she'd be pretty far out of his league. He didn't usually hang around with women who had college degrees, much less an M.D. tacked on after their names. Hell, he didn't even have a high-school diploma. Not that he missed it all that much. But women could get hung up on things like a guy's credentials. Unless they were the kind who only looked at the balance in a man's checkbook. Dr. Pam didn't seem the type.

Chewing thoughtfully, he listened to the quiet. It wouldn't be so bad to fill up the house with a wife and a bunch of kids. What was the point, after all, of parlaying a thirty-five-to-one shot into a whole breeding farm if you didn't have anyone to share it with?

Chapter Three

A kid no taller than Lucky's knees crashed into him at full speed, toppled onto the carpeting, and let out a huge squall. His mother scooped him up, taking him kicking and screaming back to the molded plastic chairs that lined the waiting room of the Inland Pediatric Clinic. The walls were covered with bright pictures and cartoon characters. One corner of the room was a giant play area overflowing with toys. Even though it was noon, there were still several mothers and their children hanging around the clinic that was located across the street from the main hospital.

Lucky adjusted the pizza box he was carrying. Didn't Dr. Pam take a lunch break? he wondered.

He went to the receptionist's window.

She closed her eyes, inhaled deeply and sighed. "Baby Cakes, if that's a new after-shave you're wearing, you're sure gonna have every woman in town chasing after you."

"Pepperoni and mushroom."

She gave him a come-hither smile. "Lunch time is definitely looking up."

"It's for the doctor."

"She ordered takeout?"

"Nope. I brought in."

The receptionist eyed him cautiously. A big woman, her skin was as dark as mahogany and her smile, bright and cheerful. Lucky wouldn't want to meet her in a mud wrestling contest, but he suspected somewhere inside the generous body lay an equally generous heart. The name tag pinned to her floral-print lab jacket identified her as Irma Sue Saunders.

"Dr. Pam know you're coming?" she asked.

"It's a surprise."

"A good or bad surprise?"

He shrugged. "If I was bringing a pizza for your lunch, Irma Sue, what would you think?"

She rolled her eyes, the whites showing around the deep brown. "I'd think you were heaven-sent."

"Let's hope the doc feels the same way."

"It's gonna be a while." She nodded toward the remaining patients. "We got a little behind schedule this morning. We always do."

"I can wait." He leaned over the counter to give her his most persuasive smile. "I'd be happy to share a slice with you if there's a way to warm this pizza when the time comes."

"Baby Cakes, I'm so hungry, I'll cook you a seven-course meal in the autoclave if you'll give me one little bite of pepperoni."

"Hey, darlin', I'll let you take a bite of anything you'd like." He opened the box to let her take a whiff.

Laughing at his salacious invitation, she levered a slice from the container with her fingers, took a sample bite and sighed again. "I do believe you are just what the doctor ordered."

"I aim to please."

"Mind you, I'm right protective of Dr. Pam. She's a fine woman and a damn good doctor."

"I wouldn't think of arguing with a woman of your obvious intelligence."

She raised her eyebrows. "I wouldn't want any Lothario trying to take advantage of her."

"Absolutely not."

She took another bite of pizza, obviously savoring the flavor. "You got any money?"

Lucky barked a laugh. "Enough to handle a pizza or two."

"Pity. Dr. Pam could use a sugar daddy about now."

"That so?"

"This clinic may be her pride and joy, but it's about to drive her to her knees from overwork and into the poor house for lack of paying customers."

"That doesn't sound very good."

"It's not. Meadowbrook needs a clinic like this, someplace where folks can bring their sick babies and not feel like they're being looked down on. Dr. Ted— that's Dr. Pam's deceased husband—was real good at glad-handing and raising money to cover the expenses of those who can't manage on their own. I think Dr.

Pam's real uncomfortable asking for handouts, even when it's for somebody else."

Lucky mentally filed that bit of information away for later use. "I'll keep that in mind, Irma Sue. *If* I come across anybody who qualifies as a sugar daddy. Maybe if you could give a few more details...."

PAM STEPPED OUT of an examining room and turned toward the adjacent one, pulling the chart for the next patient from the slot by the door. Simultaneously, her subconscious registered the scent of pizza and the sight of Lucky O'Toole at the front desk. She stopped midstride. To her dismay, her heart rate nearly doubled its pace.

What the devil was he—

Irma Sue waltzed by with a big grin on her face. "Looks like we got us man set on doin' a little courtin', Dr. Pam."

"You're welcome to him," she said grimly.

"I already got my man. You're the one who needs a little lovin' to put a smile on your face."

"I smile."

"Not ne___ ___ough, Dr. Pam. And never for the right reasons."

She smiled a lot, Pam thought defensively. She smiled at babies and toddlers and concerned moms every day, all day long. Just because there didn't happen to be a man in her life didn't mean she was wallowing in gloom or self-pity. Her work was very fulfilling. And serious.

She didn't have to go around with a sappy look on her face all the time.

Like O'Toole did.

All right, so she'd had a good time playing that game with him and Angie the prior evening. She'd laughed a lot. Smiled, too, she imagined. And hadn't been able to get the image of his teasing blue eyes out of her mind all night. But that didn't mean she was eager to see him again this afternoon.

Entering the examining room, she vowed to ignore his presence. With any luck, he'd lose interest and go away by the time she'd seen the rest of her morning patients.

She worked her way through a well-baby checkup, a mild case of bronchitis, an ear infection, and made a referral to a cardiac specialist for a two-year-old who had a disturbing arryhthmia in his heart. Unfortunately, O'Toole appeared to be a patient man.

After the waiting room had cleared out, she found him piecing together a Mickey Mouse puzzle in the play area. He was sitting in a chair designed for a five-year-old, and his long legs were folded up nearly to his chin. Everything he did exuded raw sexuality. Even when he should have looked a little silly, like now, the contrast between the small table and his large frame simply added to the aura of a man comfortable with his masculinity.

"I'm getting pretty good at this," he said, glancing up at her. His eyes swept over her in a quick appraisal that made her breath catch in her throat.

She lifted her chin, as if appearing to be determined would magically erase her all-too-intense reaction to him. "You seem to be easily amused."

"Yes, ma'am, I'm not at all hard to please." In an agile movement, he rose to his full six-feet plus. "A little friendly conversation, a few sweet words, then maybe we could get around to—"

"Why are you here?"

"I brought you lunch."

"I wasn't planning to eat lunch. I was going to check with the hospital social worker about Angie."

"What? No dinner last night, and now you're going to skip lunch? Shame, shame on you. You have to keep up your strength, Doc. Never can tell when you'll need it." The corners of his lips edged up into a broader smile. "Just in case you have to run away from a man bent on seduction."

A warm shiver purled down Pam's spine and curled through her midsection. She was about to make some smart retort—assuming her mind hadn't gone completely blank—when Irma Sue called them from the back room.

"Come on, you two. Pizza's ready. The cheese is sizzling."

The cheese wasn't the only thing sizzling. Unless Pam was undergoing an early onset of menopause, the hot flash she was experiencing was definitely sexual in origin. O'Toole had the uncanny ability to arouse her with little more than a quick smile and a few well-chosen words.

She fought back with her own verbal swords.

"If you'd use that glib Irish tongue of yours to make an honest living, you wouldn't have to rely on gambling for your livelihood."

"Doc, you just left me the biggest opening in the world to tell you what I'd like to do with my tongue. And how much you'd enjoy it. But I'm too much of a gentleman to take advantage—"

"Oh, you..." Her face on fire, Pam whirled away. The warm, deep sound of his laughter followed her down the hall while the thought of O'Toole's tongue doing incredibly erotic things to her came vividly to mind. The man was absolutely impossible! That's not what she had meant. Not at all!

Against her better judgment, Pam agreed to picnic on pizza and canned drinks with Irma Sue and O'Toole in her office. But she didn't linger.

After one slice, she excused herself. "I really do have to see Martha Dougher at the hospital before my afternoon patients arrive."

"The social worker?" O'Toole asked.

"Yes." She slipped past his chair. "You enjoy the rest of the pizza with Irma Sue. Thank you for lunch."

She never had a prayer of making it out the door without him. Somehow she'd known that. But it hadn't stopped her from trying.

"You don't need to come along, Mr. O'Toole." He matched her stride for stride across the parking lot toward the hospital. "I'm sure everything's been taken care of by the hospital."

"I'll just make sure Angie's okay. She still seemed a little anxious this morning."

"You've been in to see her?"

"You bet. It's not often a man finds a young lady who is that anxious to come home with him."

Pam shot him a glance. She imagined he was used to having any woman he wanted, from age six to sixty, groveling at his feet. "I'm hoping they've located her family by now."

"Not likely."

Inside the hospital lobby, two colorful floral bouquets sat on the information counter waiting for a volunteer to deliver them to patients upstairs. Pam headed for the Patient Services office, which was on the first floor. Martha's secretary waved her inside.

Like a persistent rash, O'Toole stuck right with her.

In addition to Martha Dougher, the Meadowbrook police chief, Larry Coleman, was in the office.

"Hello, Chief," Pam said. "How is Meadowbrook's finest?"

Smiling, he extended his hand. His bushy gray sideburns and handlebar mustache appeared to be an overcompensation for a head that was nearly bald. "Overworked and underpaid, just like you, I imagine."

"And your two grandchildren?"

"Holy terrors. I expect to see their names on the FBI's Most Wanted list by the time they're in kindergarten."

Pam laughed, then introduced O'Toole. She noted how he took the chief's hand firmly and bestowed a heart-stopping smile on Martha Dougher, who nearly swooned with pleasure. O'Toole definitely had a way with women.

"We wanted to check on Angie Rhoades," Pam said before Martha had a chance to faint dead away from the sheer joy of having a man deign to kiss her maidenly hand.

"That's why I'm here," Larry told them. "I've checked all the surrounding cities and with the county sheriff. We don't have any missing person's reports for a child matching Angie's description."

Who could have abandoned her? Pam wondered, suppressing a surge of indignant rage. Or had the child simply appeared out of some Irish mist?

"Isn't there a national clearing house for missing children?" O'Toole asked. He settled one lean hip on the edge of Martha's cluttered desk. If anything, he had on an older pair of jeans today than he had worn yesterday. The soft fabric gloved his muscular thigh like the caress of a woman's hand. And Pam was determined not to think about that.

"Yes, and I've faxed the information to Washington," the chief said. "It'll take a while to get a response."

"So you're going to leave her in the hospital?" O'Toole asked.

Martha spoke up. "Oh, no, that would be quite against hospital policy, unless Dr. Pam can certify there's a medical reason."

"There isn't." This morning Angie had seemed as healthy as any six-year-old she'd examined, except for the fact that she could use a regular, more nutritious diet. "At least, there are no serious problems I can identify." Although there was a small question of her mental health, given that she wanted to live with Lucky O'Toole. But she was young and would no doubt make other mistakes in judgment as she grew up.

"I can take her over to the county juvenile facility for you," the chief offered.

"Wait a minute." O'Toole was back on his feet. "I'll take her home with me."

"That's really not possible," Martha began.

"Why not? I'm an upstanding citizen of this county, I pay my taxes, and my house is sure big enough. There's got to be a shortage of foster homes. So, I volunteer."

"You can't just volunteer, Mr. O'Toole." Martha did her imitation of a stern social worker. "I used to work for the county. It takes at least three months to do a background check on potential foster parents. Even at that, a single gentleman..." She fluttered her nearly invisible eyelashes. "You are single, aren't you, Mr. O'Toole?"

"Absolutely."

"Then, providing foster care for a young girl who is not your relative would be most unusual. Almost unheard of. At the very least, you and the child would have to be supervised by someone of outstanding character, preferably someone who lived in the same household."

Eyes narrowing in challenge, he turned toward Pam. "How 'bout if the doc lived at my place?"

"In that case," Martha said, her age-lined face going rigid in disapproval, "I'm sure I could expedite matters."

Pam blanched. "I don't—"

The chief cleared his throat. "Congratulations, Dr. Pam. I know my wife will be real pleased to hear you've found someone—"

"No!" she protested. "I do not live with Mr. O'Toole, I have no intention of doing so, and I haven't *found* anybody."

O'Toole raised his eyebrows. "Then take her to your place. You love kids, don't you? You've got enough room, don't you? Don't let her go to a damn orphanage."

"I can't. I work long hours. I don't have a babysitter. She is *not* my responsibility." She could think of a thousand excuses not to become a foster parent for any child. But keeping as far away from O'Toole as possible was her primary need at this moment. That wouldn't be a choice if Angie was involved. He'd track them both down.

She turned to Martha. "I'll rely on you and Chief Coleman to do what is best for the child. I'll go upstairs and sign her release papers now."

She got out of the office safely. And down the hallway. But he caught up with her in the elevator.

He jammed the Stop button with the heel of his palm and trapped them between floors. Anxiety tightened a knot in Pam's midsection. They stood glowering at each other like two boxers getting ready for the bell.

"Why is Angie so important to you?" she asked, using her most clinical, calm voice, in spite of the way her insides were trembling. He was so serious, so intense, it frightened her. "If anything, she's been abandoned by her parents and needs a stabilizing influence—"

"I was raised in an orphanage, and then shuttled from one foster home to another. A kid ought to know someone wants him. Or her."

"I'm sorry." But that wasn't her problem, either. She had a clinic to run, her own family to hold together . . .

He backed her into a corner of the elevator. His distinctive brows shadowed his eyes as though he were the dark hero in some gothic romance. "What's your price, Dr. Pam?"

She swallowed hard. "Price?"

"I'll pay you to move in with me so I can have Angie, too. What'll it take? A thousand dollars a day? Two?"

Never in her life had she had such a strong urge to slap a man. Or say yes.

She stiffened her spine—and her resolve—against both his compelling Irish eyes and her own weakness. "I'm not for sale, Mr. O'Toole."

"But your clinic will be if you can't pay the bills."

Her eyes widened. How did he know that?

"I'll write you a check for whatever amount you name. Angie won't interfere with you or your clinic. I've got a housekeeper who can help if I need her, and a foreman who is great with kids, so you won't have to be bothered. But I want your assurance that you'll live with me for however long it takes for me to gain custody of Angie."

"You play the horses. How could you possibly—"

"I *own* horses, Doc. Sixteen of them earned over a million dollars in purses last year."

A million dollars. With that amount of money she could pay off all of her bills and hire a second pediatrician, too. She could make Ted's dream of a self-sufficient clinic come true with an endowment. She could actually have a few days a month when she wasn't on call. She might even be able to—

But no, she wouldn't think about that. Or the way O'Toole's eyes had darkened and seemed to bore into her psyche. Romance should be a long way from her mind. Sex even more distant. Clearly, he was discussing a business arrangement, eccentric as it might be.

"No strings attached," he assured her as though reading the wayward direction of her thoughts. "I've got six bedrooms, and you can take your pick. I won't lay a hand on you."

"I have to work. I can't supervise—"

"Martha made it clear if we were a couple—"

"We're not!"

"We can convince her that we are now. And the Child Services people, too. What I want is to provide a home for Angie. Is that so terrible?"

No. It wasn't. Though Pam hadn't intended to get drawn into the situation. "It may still be that her parents will turn up, or a legal guardian. Giving up a child you've become attached to can be very difficult."

"I don't expect that to happen, but if it does..." His brows lowered into a frown and his Adam's apple moved as though he were having difficulty swallowing. "That'd be tough."

Perhaps nothing he could have said moved Pam more than his acknowledgement that he'd hate to give up Angie once she was his. She didn't understand how he could have come to care for a child so quickly. But she didn't doubt him. Not in her heart, a part of her anatomy that had felt as dry as dust until quite recently.

"All right, I'll move in with you," she agreed cautiously, trying to think only of the child's needs and the future of Ted's clinic. "But, if for a single moment I think it's not in Angie's best interests to be living with you, I'll be gone and so will she."

His sexy grin creased his cheeks and lit his blue eyes with a teasing light. "That works for me, sweetheart. It definitely works for me."

Chapter Four

Angie leaned over the side of the hospital bed and tried to gag herself by sticking her finger down her throat. That's what the big kids did when they wanted to skip school. She figured if the social worker thought she was sick, she wouldn't be sent to the county home. Lucky and Dr. Pam would see to that. Then the three of them would have time to get to know each other and they'd pick her to be their little girl.

She coughed, but nothing much happened. How come she couldn't even get sick when she wanted to? She never got anything right.

Flopping onto her back, she hugged her brand-new teddy bear and stared up at the ceiling squares. A tear trickled out of the corner of her eye.

"Mister Saint Peter, are you still up there?"

"I'm here, Angelica."

"I thought I was going to get to pick my own parents."

"I'm still working on it, Angelica."

She lowered her eyebrows and tried to look mean, just like she did when a bully was picking on her. Only this time she was really scared. She liked Lucky. And Dr. Pam, too. But maybe they didn't like her so much. "I guess I could come back up there with you."

"I don't believe that will be necessary."

Her chin quivered. "It's hard for a kid to wait, you know."

"I know, Angelica." His voice was gentle. "You do the best you can, and I'll try to hurry things along."

A few minutes later, the door to her room opened. "Hey, sport, you ready to get outta this place?"

Angie's eyes widened as Lucky dumped a big shopping bag on the foot of her bed. "I can leave?"

"You bet. The doc has given you a clean bill of health and you're gonna come live with me."

"Forever and always?"

"For now, anyway. We'll talk about forever later. Dr. Pam is coming, too. She told me to get you some clothes to wear." He produced two pairs of jeans and some T-shirts out of the bag. "I didn't know what size you wore, but I figured these would do for now. We can all go shopping in the next couple of days and pick out stuff you like."

"Wow!" Scrambling to her knees, Angie examined everything. There was an orange T-shirt with a bright yellow flower on it, a Mickey Mouse T-shirt, and a long-sleeve shirt with polka dots. The jeans were brand-new. They even had the tags on them. She'd never, *ever* had jeans that weren't hand-me-downs.

At the bottom of the shopping bag there was a sweatshirt, and slippery silk underpants with butterflies and ballerinas, and three new pairs of white socks to go with a pair of red tennis shoes. "Wow!" she said again.

She started to yank off her hospital gown so she could try everything on, then stopped abruptly. "Thank you."

"You're welcome, sport. It was my pleasure." Lucky smiled at her just like a daddy should.

"I didn't mean to be greedy," she assured him solemnly, remembering Saint Peter's warning.

"Hey, every young lady has a right to get excited about new clothes. Can you get dressed by yourself, or do you need somebody to help you?"

"I can do it." She thought about telling him she had been dressing herself for a long time, but decided that might not be polite. Instead, she remembered her manners and added another, "Thank you." Gosh, it was going to be hard to be good *all* the time.

"Okay, I'll wait for you out in the hall. You come find me when you're ready to go."

Lucky slipped out the door. Angie was definitely a cute kid. Well behaved. Good manners. This being a father didn't look as if it'd be too hard.

He spotted Pam at the nurses' station and he strolled in that direction.

"Everything all set?" he asked.

Before responding, she watched the passage of a youngster on a gurney, her expression solemn, then turned her attention to a patient chart. "I'm just signing off on Angie's chart. Did you get her some clothes?"

"Yep. She's changing now." He edged a little closer and caught the sweet scent of roses. With her head bent over the chart, Pam's hair had slid forward. He resisted the urge to tuck the soft curl behind her ear and maybe run his fingertips along the curve of her jaw. Instead, he jammed his hands in his pockets. "You get your other patients taken care of?"

"Irma Sue canceled a couple of appointments for me, and we referred a sore throat to the local ear, nose and throat man. I don't like having to ask other doctors to fill in for me."

"Why not? You'd do it for them, wouldn't you?"

"Of course."

"Then what's the big deal?"

Turning, she leveled him a look like the one the nuns used to give him when he'd been talking in the back of the room. "Mr. O'Toole, I am feeling very uncomfortable about the decision I made. It has caused me to ignore the needs of my patients."

"You saw to it they were taken care of."

"Furthermore, moving in with a man whom I have just met strikes me as the epitome of foolishness."

"Yeah," he drawled. "We're gonna have a lot of fun getting acquainted, aren't we?"

She responded with a frown. "I'm having serious second thoughts."

"Except about the clinic. You need my dough to keep the clinic going."

A tinge of pink colored her cheeks. She wasn't the kind of woman who wore much makeup, and a blush looked good on her. "My husband—"

"Too bad I never met this paragon of virtue you keep talking about. I'd have told him his wife needed to have more fun in her life. A few laughs now and then." He leaned a little closer and lowered his voice. "A few more rolls in the hay."

The ballpoint pen in her hand snapped. "Mr. O'Toole, if you are trying to irritate me—"

"Irritation is not what you're feeling."

"I could slap you."

"But you won't. You're a real lady. Besides, you're curious."

"About what, for heaven's sake?"

"About how we'd be together." He carefully extracted the broken pen from her fingertips. "We'd be hot, Doc. Sizzling."

"We would not—"

"But I'm not going to jump your bones, Doc. I promise. I'm only interested in making a home for Angie."

As if on cue, Angie appeared out of her room. Her jeans were so long they folded under her feet, her bright orange T-shirt reached her knees. In her hand she carried the shopping bag like a determined, though junior-size bag lady.

Pam choked down a hysterical laugh. She was caught in a web woven by an adorable child and a madman, both of whom made her feel things she had no right to be feeling. A crazy quilt of wanting to be a woman, a mother and a lover all at once. None of that made sense, yet she was helpless to resist their attraction. It was as if a force outside her control was acting on her. And she was responding. Her knees felt weak, her heart dangerously light.

She struggled to maintain some semblance of sanity in a world suddenly turned upside down.

"I gather you lack experience in selecting children's clothing," she said. The corners of her lips twitched as she fought to repress a smile.

He shot her a wicked grin and shrugged. "Maybe I should have taken a few measurements first." His blue eyes sparkled with amusement as he met her gaze.

In spite of her best efforts, she lost it. How in the name of heaven could she keep a straight face when he was so tickled with himself? She tipped back her head and laughed. Out loud. The sound seemed rusty with disuse.

From behind the counter, the floor nurse asked, "Are you all right, Dr. Pam?"

"Of course, I am." Oddly enough, she did feel fine. Maybe better than she had in a long time.

Somehow she managed to get Angie's pant legs rolled up enough so the child could walk without tripping over the cuffs.

"I have to stop by my place to pack a suitcase if I'm going to move in with you," she told O'Toole as the three of them left the hospital. From the corner of her eye, Pam caught a puzzled look from the volunteer receptionist at the front desk. She stifled a groan. If she wasn't careful, her professional image would soon be in tatters. A doctor couldn't risk losing the respect of her patients.

Angie slipped her hand into Pam's. "I'd like to see your house, Dr. Pam. I bet it's real pretty."

"Actually, it's a town house, Angie. Not a house house." Ted had decided, given their busy schedules, a maintenance-free town house was the most practical choice. Pam had always assumed once they had children they'd buy a home with more space, which had been her preference from the beginning. Of course, since she had never gotten pregnant, the issue hadn't been discussed again.

"Okay, you take the kid with you," O'Toole agreed amiably. He gave Pam directions to his house that would take them to a rural part of the county, then said, "I'll go warn Rafael we've got company coming."

He tossed the shopping bag into the cab of a pickup that appeared to be on its last legs. A fender was missing and the paint on the rest of the truck so faded, Pam wasn't sure what the original color might have been. It made her seriously question O'Toole's assertion that he'd made millions on his stable of horses. From the appearance of the truck, she doubted the vehicle could even make it as far as the nearest racetrack. And the owner wouldn't be able to afford a two-dollar bet.

As though he had noted her questioning look, he said, "My other car is in the paint shop. It got a few scratches in the accident." He winked. "It's a Ferrari. You'll love riding with the top down."

"I'm sure." She didn't want to think about a sleek sports car, the wind blowing in her face, and a sexy devil-may-care Irishman at the wheel. But she did. And the image was distressingly appealing.

VIEWED FROM A CHILD'S perspective, Pam guessed her town house would hold little attraction. The furniture was a little too formal, the rooms too tidy. On every horizontal surface there were expensive knickknacks, souvenirs from trips she and Ted had taken together or gifts from friends. Outside, the minuscule yard offered no space for a child to play, either.

Suddenly, her home felt claustrophobic, and Pam was anxious to be on her way to Lucky's farm. An odd feeling, really, since at some very deep level she knew he was the man she most wanted to avoid.

"You can watch television while I pack," she suggested to Angie. "Or would you rather have a snack?" Not that Pam kept much in the way of food in the house. Her meal planning was very basic, and she often skipped dinner if she was too tired to prepare something.

"I'll just look around. If that's okay." Angie gazed up at her solemnly. "I won't touch anything."

Smiling, Pam smoothed the child's disorderly bangs. "Whatever you'd like is fine."

She went upstairs to her bedroom, retrieved a suitcase from the back of the closet and was checking her wardrobe for clothes that would be suitable for a horse-breeding farm when she heard a crash. A sharp, shattering sound.

Wincing, her first thought was that Angie might have hurt herself.

Racing downstairs, she found Angie in the dining room staring wide eyed at the broken fragments of a terra-cotta statuette that had crashed onto the decorative tile floor.

Angie's chin trembled. "I'm sorry. I didn't mean to break it. Honest, I didn't."

Pam eyed the child for a moment. This particular piece had been on display in the living room, not the dining room. Someone had carried it into this room, and thrown, not dropped it to the floor. "It's all right, honey," she said, trying to dismiss her suspicions. She knelt and began picking up the broken shards. "It never did me any good, anyway."

"It looked like a doll. I just wanted to hold it a minute."

"It was a fertility doll I bought in Egypt."

"Fertility? What's that mean?"

"It means that a woman wants to try and have a baby," Pam explained, hoping that would be enough to satisfy her six-year-old mind.

"Was it expensive?"

"No, the vendor had a whole table full of them. I made my husband buy one for me as a joke." Though Ted hadn't laughed, as she recalled. Nor had she. In fact, she'd taken the whole thing too seriously. After they returned home, Pam had stroked the doll's fat belly almost daily for months—a foolishly futile act.

"Are you gonna send me away because I broke it?"

Pam slid the child a look. "No, I'm not. But I would like you to be more careful in the future." And more honest, too. Something was afoot here she couldn't quite fathom.

A cherubic look of relief swept over Angie's face. "Then can I come upstairs and watch you pack? That way I won't get into any more trouble."

Pam laughed. She had the oddest feeling trouble followed Angie around like a twin sister wherever she went, upstairs or down, and she wondered if Lucky was prepared to deal with that in the same *skillful* way he'd handled buying clothes for the child.

It didn't take long for Pam to pack. Mostly personal items—toothbrush, shampoo, blow dryer, plus a couple of changes of clothes. She'd be able to drop by whenever she needed anything more.

Driving out of town, Pam followed Lucky's directions and slowed the car as she tried to catch the numbers on the rural mailboxes. The road wound its way through gently rolling countryside, the hills dotted with stately California live oaks. A narrow creek meandered along the valley floor, passing under—and sometimes over—the roadway at several low spots. So far, the season had been relatively dry and everyone was hoping the drought wouldn't return. Or the unexpected floods from rain-swollen creeks that had plagued the area last year. A year of *average* rainfall would be a blessing.

The four-leaf clover painted on the mailbox gave the place away even before Pam could read the address. She turned into the drive. Her breath lodged in her lungs as she looked up the hill.

A huge white house was perched on a knoll surrounded by fields of lush grass. In rolling checkerboard fashion, fences traveled across the slopping terrain like precisely drawn chalk lines, separating mares and their colts from grazing stallions and spry yearlings from their younger siblings.

To call this a farm was a serious understatement, Pam realized. *Estate* was a far better description.

"Wow! I knew it'd be great!" Angie exclaimed. She squirmed under the constraint of her seat belt to get a better view. "Look at all those horses! There's zillions of them. You think Lucky will let me ride one? Do you, huh?"

"I don't know, honey. They look like pretty expensive animals to me." And far too large and powerful for a child to ride.

She parked in front of the house just as Lucky was coming down the steps. Angie didn't wait for an invitation. She fumbled excitedly with her seat belt and leaped out of the car almost before it had come to a full stop and raced toward the nearest horse, a mare in a field by herself.

Worried about the child's safety, Pam hurried after her. Lucky, with a burst of speed worthy of a world-class sprinter, beat her to the fence Angie was already climbing.

"Easy, kid, don't spook the horse," he warned. He clamped his hand firmly, yet gently on Angie's shoulder.

"I just wanted to pet him." Extending her hand, Angie leaned over the fence. The horse shied away with a few quick steps that made her dark mane shimmer.

"It's a her," Lucky explained. "A filly named Sweet Sigh. She's a little high-strung."

"She's beautiful," Pam said. Boosting herself up by stepping on the lowest rung of the fence, she rested her forearms along the top. Inadvertently, her arm brushed against Lucky's. In spite of the cool afternoon air, his skin was warm. Very warm.

"She's fast, too," he said. "She's the only horse I've ever owned that actually had a shot at the Kentucky Derby, and a filly at that. She loves to run with the boys." He cocked Pam one of his seductive half smiles. "Some women are like that, I understand."

"I wouldn't know." She studiously averted her gaze. "Where did you get the name Sweet Sigh?"

"Comes from the sweetest sound a man can ever hear."

Not understanding, she looked at him questioningly.

"From a woman who has been well satisfied. Definitely a sweet sigh," Lucky whispered for Pam's ears only.

At the instant of understanding, heat started low in her body and curled upward in an increasing spiral until the flame touched Pam's cheeks. "I'm sorry I asked," she said between clenched teeth.

"I'd be happy to demonstrate."

"That won't be necessary."

"The time and place of your choosing, naturally."

"I choose to decline. Thanks anyway."

"I'll keep the offer open. In case you change your mind."

"I won't."

"We'll see."

Stepping down from the fence, Pam discovered her knees were slightly weak and wobbly, like a foal who hadn't quite gotten the hang of walking yet. O'Toole and his persistent innuendos had a decided effect on her. Or maybe it was her own vivid imagination that was playing havoc with her equilibrium.

Gazing longingly at the horse in the paddock, Angie asked, "Can I ride her, Lucky? She looks real gentle."

"Not Sweet Sigh, sport. She's a racehorse. It takes a real jockey to handle her."

"Have you gots another horse then? One that a little kid can ride?"

He frowned. "I don't think so. We'll have to ask Rafael."

"But that's why—" Angie clamped her mouth shut.

"Come on, let's get you two settled in and we can have dinner." Lucky snared the child around the waist and tossed her potato-sack style over his shoulder. She giggled, the momentary tension that had appeared in her eyes vanishing as quickly as it had come.

As Pam trailed along behind the two of them, she told herself everything was going to be fine. This strange arrangement would last only a few days, no more than a week, Pam was sure. Lucky would make a generous contribution to the clinic, Angie would be restored to her rightful family, and Pam would be able to resume her normal life.

Inside the house, Lucky sent Angie upstairs to search for whichever bedroom she would like to be hers. Following along behind the child's eager footsteps, he delivered Pam's suitcase to a room with an incredible view. Grassy hillsides rolled down to the creek below, then oak trees marched up the opposite side of the canyon. In the distance, only the tips of the highest hills were still touched by the setting sun, leaving the rest silhouetted in a deep purple.

"So this is how the other half lives," she said in admiration of both the house and the view.

"As they say, being obscenely rich is a tough job, but somebody has to do it." He placed her suitcase on a queen-size bed covered with a velvet spread in a soft shade of mauve. "Of course, a couple of wrong guesses on my part about which horse ought to run in which race could wipe me out in a hurry. Or something as simple as a contagious disease could decimate the stables overnight. Horse racing can be a pretty iffy business, particularly since the government made the tax laws less attractive."

"Doesn't the risk bother you?"

"Not particularly. I like having a big house and some folding money in my wallet, but if I had to start over again it wouldn't be the end of the world."

"Personally, I like to know I can write a check and it won't bounce." Though financial ups and downs had never appeared to bother the rest of Pam's family. Until Ted's death, she'd assumed she'd have the kind of security she craved.

From down the hall, Angie called, "Lucky! Dr. Pam! I found the room I want. Come quick!"

"I think it would be better not to spoil Angie too much," Pam warned. "When they locate her parents—"

"You'd get more out of life if you didn't cross bridges before you got to them, Doc," he countered with a wink, then hurried out the door in response to another excited cry from Angie.

"If someone doesn't plan ahead, no one gets around to *building* any bridges," she called after his departing figure.

LUCKY WAS CONTENT.

His stomach was full from a hastily concocted spaghetti dinner. In spite of a wind that had kicked up outside, the house was warm. And there was a beautiful woman sitting curled up at the far end of the couch in his TV room, leafing through medical journals.

He had seen the instinctive way she touched Angie at odd moments and how her concerned gaze followed a young patient on a gurney being transported through the hospital corridors. Those simple gestures spoke more eloquently of the depth of her feelings than her professional facade. He suspected she was a woman capable of great love who had decided to hide her emotions beneath a more stern veneer.

His forehead tightened into a thoughtful frown. Maybe he wasn't all that content, now that he'd given the idea some serious consideration.

Angie had gone off to bed almost an hour ago and Pam hadn't said one word since. She'd had her nose buried in that darn magazine the whole time. Technical stuff, he imagined. Bone dry and boring.

Meanwhile, Lucky had been thinking about the way she tucked her legs up under her, leaving her bare toes peeking out. And how the sweater she wore made a man's fingers itch to test the soft texture of cashmere and feel the swell of her breasts. He kept wondering how she would taste if he got a chance to kiss her. Sweet, he imagined. And hot.

Noisily adjusting his position in the upholstered chair opposite her, he waited for Pam to look up. Her eyes were such a striking shade of brown, they made him think of rich, warm chocolate. When she had smiled at Angie during dinner, her full lips curving with just a hint of pleasure, Lucky's heart had twisted with the desire that she smile at him in the same way.

Given how she'd reacted to him a time or two, Lucky suspected she wasn't as immune to his charms as she tried to let on.

He cleared his throat.

That got her attention. Her luscious brown eyes focused on him. He liked that. A lot.

"What do you think we ought to do about it?" he asked.

"Do about what?"

"This mutual attraction we're feeling for each other."

"Mutual—" she sputtered. "Dream on, O'Toole."

"I admit, just because there's a thousand degrees worth of passion simmering beneath the surface here, we don't have to act on it. We both have our reputations to maintain."

"A thousand—" She slapped her magazine shut. "Are you saying that if we slept together, I'd ruin *your* reputation?" Pam knew she should get up and leave the room—leave the house, for that matter. His comments were way out of line. But she didn't budge. Because the truth was, she'd been thinking about exactly the same topic. Sleeping with Lucky. Making love with Lucky. Sating her desire with the one man she shouldn't even be considering as a romantic partner.

"I'm just saying," he continued so nonchalantly it set Pam's teeth on edge, "that you don't have to be afraid of me."

"I'm not."

"Good. Then you won't mind if I kiss you."

Her eyes widened. "I most certainly do mind."

"You've been trained as a scientist. It seems to me, an experiment is in order. We can kiss once, and get it out of our systems, or we can keep wondering what it would be like."

Why did that sound so logical? There was a flaw there somewhere, but she couldn't seem to identify what that might be when she was looking into those bright blue Irish eyes of his. Concentrating at all seemed impossibly difficult. And not particularly appealing.

Fatigue tugged at the back of her mind. It had been a long day. Maybe if she closed her eyes, just for an instant, she could figure out why Lucky's proposition didn't make any sense at all.

Opening her eyes, she found him sitting next to her on the couch. Very close. So close she caught the scent of his spicy after-shave and a fragrance that had to be pure masculinity. A little tuft of dark hair peeped out above the V of his sport shirt. He was saying something, but the pounding beat of her heart muted his words.

"An experiment?" she questioned.

"Very scientific."

"Once?"

"A reasonable test, given the circumstances."

"Sort of like academic research?"

"Absolutely," he said in a husky voice as he lowered his head toward hers. The moment their lips touched, Pam knew once would never be enough. His mouth was too inviting, too persuasive by far. For the first time in her life, she felt such a strong, swift rising of desire, it took her breath away. Indeed, she thought she might never breathe again. Might never want to.

He slid his palm along the column of her neck, tunneled his fingers through her hair, and she shivered, though not from the cold. Instead, the heat from his touch melted some deeply buried defense mechanism she'd desperately clung to for years.

Lifting his head, his breathing labored, he said, "I'm not sure our experiment proved what we wanted it to."

"Of course it did," she lied. Her heart beat as if it had experienced a vigorous aerobic workout. "It's good we got that out of our systems. Terrific, in fact." She forced a smile.

With all the self-discipline she could muster, she extricated herself from the couch and Lucky's tempting blue eyes. "I expect to be working very long hours the next few days, but I'm sure you'll take good care of Angie."

Her workdays wouldn't be a problem, Pam realized. She could avoid contact with Lucky from dawn until long past dusk, if she wanted. It was the weekends, when she'd be forced to deal directly with him again, that would pose the far greater challenge.

Chapter Five

On Saturday, the first morning she allowed herself to sleep in, Pam discovered she'd been right. The weekends were going to put a severe strain on her ability to keep her distance from Lucky and the fanciful dreams he somehow managed to conjure in her thoughts.

The moment she stepped out of the spacious guest bedroom, Angie's high-pitched giggles and Lucky's rich, warm laughter drew her toward the kitchen. It was a family sound, the carefree timbre of people with no concerns, no troubles to darken their mood. Or at least none they were willing to acknowledge.

Pam paused at the open kitchen door.

Who would have guessed there was that much flour in the world? Angie was covered with it, and Lucky hadn't fared much better. His dark hair had gone gray, offering a hint of what a distinguished-looking man he'd become as he aged. Pam had to stop herself from wondering what fortunate woman would grow old with him.

"Are you two always this messy in the morning?" she asked. "Or is this a special occasion?"

"We're making pancakes." Kneeling on a chair at the kitchen table, Angie stirred a glutinous mixture of flour and who knew what else. "Lucky says you work too hard and we need to make you somethin' special. We were gonna bring you breakfast in bed."

"Were you?" Her gaze swept over him. No man had a right to look that good in the morning. He was wearing low-slung jeans that hugged impossibly lean hips. His short-sleeve shirt hung open, revealing a well-muscled chest darkened by swirling hair. Whiskers shadowed his firm jaw.

Clearly, celibacy was detrimental to her mental health. Ever since she'd moved into Lucky's house three days ago, she'd been fantasizing about him. And his kisses. He'd invaded her dreams and disturbed her concentration at work. That wasn't like her at all. With renewed resolve she shook her wayward thoughts aside.

"It's sweet of you to think of me," she said. "But I'd just as soon eat down here."

"You don't like to laze around in bed?" Lucky asked, raising his beautifully sculpted eyebrows.

"Not particularly. It seems like a waste of time."

"Depends on who you're in bed with, I suppose."

He said it straight-faced, but Pam knew what he was talking about. And who he had in mind. She didn't give him the satisfaction of seeing her blush.

"Here, Angie, let me give you a hand." Pam scooped up the bowl and stirring spoon. "We can take all this over to the sink where it will be easier to clean up the mess.''

''Hey, she walks and talks like a doctor, and she can cook, too,'' Lucky commented, stepping back out of her way.

''Just because I've let you handle the cooking the past few nights, doesn't mean I can't manage the job when I need to.''

''I can't reach the counter, Dr. Pam,'' Angie complained. She hopped down and trudged after her.

''Bring your chair. Or maybe Lucky has a small step stool.''

Pam got things cleaned up and organized in short order. She remembered how she had taught her sister Sandy to cook this same way working together at the kitchen counter. Their mother hadn't been interested in passing along what few domestic skills she had mastered. That responsibility had fallen on Pam's shoulders, as had so many others.

Not that Sandy had retained any of the lessons. Pam suspected her kid sister relied primarily on fast-food restaurants for the meals she served her adorable children.

''Lucky took me to the racetrack yesterday,'' Angie announced as Pam helped her drizzle the lumpy batter onto the griddle. ''We got to watch some horses practice running around and around the track.''

''And did you enjoy that?''

''Sure. 'Cept I wished I could ride one of the horses, too. But Lucky said no.''

Smart man, Pam thought. She glanced at him across the room. He seemed quite engrossed in watching their culinary efforts. "If Angie is going to be living here for a while, we probably should get her enrolled in school."

"I don't wanna go to school," Angie complained.

"You'd have friends your own age to play with."

"I gots a new friend. His name's José and he's twelve years old. His grandpa works for Lucky and sometimes lets José and me brush the horses."

"Why don't we wait on the school business until after the holidays?" Lucky suggested. He was leaning laconically against the far counter, his arms folded across his chest and one booted foot crossed over the other. The hint of a smile tilted the corners of his lips. "There's only two weeks left until the Christmas break."

Angie gasped. "Is there really only two weeks till Christmas?"

"Three until Christmas day," Pam explained. "Let's not rush the season any more than we have to. I still have a lot of shopping to do."

Angie's face puckered into a frown. "I've got somethin' important I've gotta do by Christmas, too." She exhaled a deep sigh.

Grasping her little hand, Pam helped her to flip the pancakes on the griddle. She seemed like such a troubled child, Pam could only hope the mystery of her missing family could be resolved soon. Though they couldn't be such great parents, considering they'd apparently abandoned her.

Pam wished she could wrap her arms around Angie and never let her go. She'd felt that way about any number of her patients, those with parents who didn't deserve the title. Obviously, the ability to procreate didn't guarantee a corresponding ability to love and nurture a child.

But in law, and in fact, she had no right to interfere in family relationships unless outright abuse was occurring. So she'd learned to keep her emotions in check, much like the little Dutch boy of storybook fame, who kept his thumb in the dike. She knew if she ever let go, and allowed her tears to flow, she might not be able to call them back.

AFTER A QUESTIONABLE repast of lumpy pancakes smothered in maple syrup, Pam helped with the cleanup, then fled out to the horse barns. She needed to be away from both Lucky and Angie, from the incessant feeling that the three of them were a family. At any moment, Chief Coleman would locate the child's missing parents or guardians. Pam knew the wisest course was not to become emotionally attached. Letting go of someone you loved was far harder than not loving at all.

And, in spite of Lucky's efforts at seduction, Pam knew she was a temporary member of his household only because he wanted to provide a home for Angie. There was no basis at all for a long-term relationship between Pam and Lucky.

She wandered along a row of recently painted stalls, each one with a half door open to let in light and air.

Rafael, Lucky's foreman, was standing at the end of the row, working on some tack. His gnarled fingers moved agilely over the leather.

"Good morning, *señora*. It is a lovely day, no?"

"It certainly is." The sky was a glorious shade of blue, the crisp morning air heavy with the scent of hay and leather. The combination reminded her of Lucky. Very masculine and strangely appealing.

"It is good you are taking a day off."

"Unlike your employer, I have to work for a living."

He raised dark eyebrows liberally sprinkled with gray. "I think you are mistaken, *señora*. Lucky is the one who works the hardest on this farm. He knows each of the horses and which mares will produce the best babies, those that will be able to run like the wind. Every foal learns his voice along with the scent of their mothers. He spends much time grooming and training the horses himself so they will know they are loved."

"I thought he was more a gambler than a horse trainer."

"When he was a boy, he slept with the horses because he had nowhere else. He learned their language and now they speak to him."

"Giving him tips on the next race, I suppose?" She asked the question tartly because she didn't want to consider too carefully that any adolescent—particularly a man like Lucky to whom she was so strongly drawn—would have ever had to sleep in a barn.

The old man produced a smile that revealed one missing tooth. "He never says so, but I think it is possible. He is a very lucky man." The horse in the stall next to Rafael stuck his nose out and begged for attention with a head bob. "There, you see? Even the mention of Lucky's name is familiar to the horse. They respond to him as they do to few other humans. If he had not grown so big and tall, Lucky would have made a fine jockey."

"He rode, too?" He'd done everything possible to survive, and done it well, she suspected.

"As a boy, yes. But no more. It is better such a smart man owns the horses and breeds them to be the very best."

Pam had the distinct impression Rafael would wax on indefinitely about Lucky's virtues if she allowed him to. It wasn't something she wanted to hear. She was already far too attracted to the man on a physical level. She didn't want to add admiration for what an orphan had done with his life. Or how she found his growing relationship with Angie so endearing. Compassion was something she simply couldn't afford when it came to Lucky. That feeling could too easily slip into love. Then she'd truly be lost, with no hope of keeping her well-defended heart in tact.

LATER THAT MORNING, Angie put her stool next to Hot Diggity and climbed up with a brush in her hand. He was a big horse with a black mane and a tail he liked to swish around, mostly when flies bothered him. Rafael let her groom the gelding if José was with her and she promised to be real, real careful.

"How do you get a girl to like a boy?" she asked her new friend. José was kinda skinny and not very tall. He tried to act big, but Angie had already figured out he was mostly scared 'cause his mom had sent him to live with his grandpa and he wasn't sure when he'd get to see her again.

"I don't know." He rubbed Hot Diggity's nose and the horse snorted.

"Don't you have a girlfriend?"

"Naw. I don't like girls yet."

"Not even me?"

"You're just a little kid. That's different."

She frowned. She didn't really like anybody calling her a little kid, but she didn't want to get into an argument with José. She needed his help.

"So what would you do if you wanted a girl to like you?"

Walking around to the horse's hind end, he lifted one of Hot Diggity's legs and began scraping out the junk that was in his hoof. "I'd talk to her, I guess."

Angie knew Lucky already talked to Dr. Pam. Lots. It didn't seem to be doing any good. The two parents Angie wanted most in the whole, entire world weren't getting together. Saint Peter was falling down on the job. Or else he was super slow. With only three weeks to go till Christmas, Angie figured she'd better start helping things along.

"What else?" she persisted. As she brushed Hot Diggity, his back muscles rippled and dust floated up from his coat because he'd been rolling around in the dirt. Angie sneezed. She sure hoped the asthma she'd had when she'd been just a baby wasn't going to come back.

"How should I know? In the movies, the guy brings his girl a dumb bouquet of flowers, or somethin'. And maybe they go out to dinner. There's candles and wine. Stuff like that. Afterward, you know, they get it on."

"Hmm." Angie didn't have any money to pay for Lucky to take Pam out to dinner, or to buy flowers. All she had was the $2.57 she'd won playing cards with Lucky. But she'd seen some candles in a drawer in the kitchen. Pretty white ones, sort of angelic looking. And there was a bottle of wine in the refrigerator. Maybe if she made something special for them, they'd get it on together . . . whatever that meant.

HE HADN'T MEANT to stalk her.

All morning Lucky had watched Pam explore his farm—in an all too apparent effort to avoid him. Now she'd wandered up the hill on the opposite side of the canyon, walking among the live oaks dusty with a summer's worth of grime. The sparse undergrowth of grass was a golden brown and had gone to seed.

He wondered what she was thinking. And wished she was thinking about him.

He'd learned a long time ago he could have almost any woman he wanted by simply crooking his finger. Money, he realized, attracted women like bees to honey. It hadn't taken him long to grow tired of that particular game.

Pam was different. Sure, she'd gone along with his scheme because she needed money for her clinic. But she hadn't needed *him*.

At some very deep level, that irritated the hell out of him. He sensed that once Pam committed herself to anything—including a man—her loyalty would be unswerving. That's why she hadn't let go of her attachment to her husband, even after all this time. And another man would be darn lucky if he could convince her to give that same determined devotion to him.

"So what's the verdict?" he asked when he had nearly caught up with her. "Do you approve?"

Her head snapped around. "I didn't hear you coming."

"Sorry. If you want to be alone, I'll go on back—"

"No, that's not necessary. I was just doing a little exploring. This whole canyon seems very private."

"Yeah, it can be real peaceful out here. Guess that's why I bought the place a few years back."

"It reminds me of where I grew up."

"I would have taken you for a city girl. High-rises. Busy streets. Lots of action."

She smiled wistfully. Dressed in jeans, a sweater and sensible shoes, she had shed some of her professional aura and appeared more approachable, subtly more feminine. Substantially more desirable, he mused, though he didn't know how that was possible. He simply thought she looked *right* here in his canyon.

"When I was about five, my parents moved us to a place in Topanga Canyon," she said. "That's in the hills above Malibu. It's almost in the middle of the city, but at the same time it can be very rural. The residents are an eclectic mix of the very wealthy and the truly eccentric.''

''Where did your folks fit in?''

Hesitating, she plucked a blade of winter brown grass and stripped the seeds. Her family was a topic she rarely discussed, but it seemed ungracious not to respond to a direct question. ''They qualify pretty high up on the eccentric scale.''

''At least you had parents.'' He said the words without bitterness, as though over the years he had accepted the fact he had been orphaned. Pam wondered how deeply one would have to probe to find the pain that must still linger somewhere inside him.

''You're right. And they loved us—my sister, brother and me. I've never doubted that. In that regard, I was very fortunate.''

He ducked under a branch to step closer. ''But eccentric isn't your bag?''

Almost every night during her adolescence, she had gone to bed praying to wake up as part of a ''normal'' family. She was well into adulthood before she learned to accept her parents' personality quirks, and she still wasn't entirely comfortable with the idea of her family being different. ''I put myself through college and med school, Lucky. That's how important it was to me to have a normal, stable life and career.''

''Your folks didn't help out at all?''

"Financially, they couldn't. I worked part-time and made up the rest with student loans. Like most doctors, when I finished my residency I was in debt up to my eyeballs."

He narrowed his gaze. "Let me guess—your paragon of a husband paid off all your bills."

"Well, yes, but if you're implying that's why I married—"

"I wasn't."

"Well, don't. Ted and I had a very good, very loving relationship."

"I'm glad. I can tell you're the kind of woman who deserves the very best." He edged closer, moving inside her personal space, snaring her with his penetrating blue eyes like a predator paralyzes his prey just before pouncing. "I do find it interesting that you're so defensive about your husband. He's been dead now...how long?"

She swallowed hard and her tongue darted out to lick lips gone suddenly dry. "Three years."

"You're determined to keep his memory alive and untarnished."

"Are you criticizing my loyalty to a man I loved?"

"Nope. Not at all. Loyalty is definitely a virtue in a woman. But I just kinda wonder if it's not time you moved on with your life."

The prospect seemed all too tempting with Lucky standing so close. From this angle she could see squint lines at the corners of his eyes, etched there by a thousand smiles, repeated almost daily. She suspected his childhood had been difficult, yet his resilience over-shadowed everything else. An admirable quality.

But he was the wrong man. Whatever his wealth, however hard he might work, he could lose it all with little more than the snap of his fingers. And he didn't seem to care.

"I have my life organized in a way that makes me comfortable, Mr. O'Toole. I'm not looking to change anything at the moment."

"No? That's a real shame. 'Cause I think you've got an itch you're just dying to scratch."

She bristled. "Not with you, I'm not."

"We'll see." He lifted his shoulders in an easy, infu-riating shrug. "Let's go see if we can rustle up some lunch. I'm starved."

"I FIXED IT all myself." Angie stood proudly beside the dining room table grinning up at Lucky and Pam. The blinds were pulled and three places were set. On each plate rested a hot dog on a bun slathered in mustard and a pile of potato chips, contrasting nicely with the crys-tal wine glasses provided for their beverage. One glass was filled to the brim with milk.

"Lunch," Lucky said.

"I haven't entirely digested the breakfast pancakes yet," Pam said under her breath. She swallowed back an amused smile.

Angie clambered into one of the chairs. "I gots to light the candles. I wanted to wait till you got back so's I didn't waste 'em, or start a fire, or anything like that."

"This must be a very special occasion," Pam commented. The candles, stuck in ornate silver holders, were the emergency variety every household should have in case of a power outage, plain white and rather stubby.

"Here, let me help you, sport." Lucky dutifully struck a match and lit both candles. "This is great. I never would have thought of having candles for lunch."

"It's s'posed to be romantic. So's you and Dr. Pam can get it on."

Pam choked. "I really don't think—"

"If you ladies would care to take your seats..." Lucky flipped a paper napkin over his arm, wine-steward style, and deftly lifted the cork from the bottle. "I would be happy to pour."

Angie giggled. "I'm not big enough to drink *wine*, Lucky."

His eyes widened in mock surprise. "You're not?"

"Nuh-uh. I'm s'posed to have milk."

"As you wish, madam." He bowed slightly, then poured a sparkling rosé into Pam's glass.

"I don't usually drink wine with lunch," she said, holding her hand up to ward him off. A futile effort, she realized. For Lucky, this was the equivalent of a child's tea party. He was playing a game. They'd slipped down Alice's hole, and Pam had little choice but to go along. In some ways, his lighthearted, almost childish attitude freed her to relax, too.

"Ah, but we must make an exception today since our hostess has gone to such pains to make our meal so tempting." He lifted his glass of wine and gave her a Cheshire cat grin. "To getting it on, my dear."

Returning his toast, she said, "Off with your head, O'Toole." But she couldn't manage a very stern look. Not even close. Instead she felt slightly giddy and seriously off balance well before she'd taken the first fruity sip of wine.

The hot dog was ice cold and uncooked, but so smothered in mustard Pam assumed any straying bacteria couldn't possibly survive. O'Toole told outrageous jokes, all of them suitable for the ears of a six-year-old. And Pam laughed. More than she had in a good many years.

She was lingering over a second glass of wine when Angie volunteered to clean up the dishes.

"You fixed lunch, honey," Pam said. "The least we can do is handle the cleanup."

"No. I want to. Honest." She glanced from Pam to Lucky and back again. "You two can keep on talking."

With far more expertise than a six-year-old should have, Angie cleared the table and vanished into the kitchen, the swinging door closing behind her.

"She's certainly going out of her way to get us together," Pam commented.

"Maybe she knows something we don't."

"I think she just desperately wants to please us. Children who have been deprived of love often act that way."

"If I could get my hands on her parents..." His thought trailed off as he studied the clear liquid in his wineglass.

"It never stops hurting, does it?" she asked softly. "Having Angie in the house reminds you of your own past and being an orphan."

He raised his gaze to meet hers. As though a curtain had been raised, she could see the depth of his pain and she knew behind his glib Irish charm there was a lifetime of loneliness. "How did you know?"

Her heart went out to him and she reached across the table to squeeze his hand. "Because that's how any normal person would feel."

Stroking his thumb over the back of her hand, he said, "I don't think about it often. There's no point."

"I know." That didn't stop her from wishing she could ease the loneliness and feelings of abandonment that still lingered in his heart.

From the kitchen, Angie screamed. "Lucky! Come quick! Something's wrong!"

They both bolted from their chairs.

Angie was standing on her step stool staring aghast at a soggy mess of mustard-tinted water and leftover buns rising in the kitchen sink. Both sides were filled nearly to overflowing.

"The water won't go down!" she cried.

"Here. Let me see." Lucky reached into the mess and felt around for the stopper, coming up empty-handed.

"Your plumbing must have backed up." Pam put a soothing arm around Angie and found that the child was shaking. "It's all right, honey. I'm sure Lucky can get it fixed."

He frowned and tried switching on the disposal. It growled threateningly.

"What'd you put down in here?" he asked.

"Just the stuff from lunch." Angie's voice quavered. "The candles wouldn't come out of the holders very good, so I ran hot water over 'em. They melted and ran down—"

"You put *candle wax* down the disposal?" he bellowed.

Pam winced. "Calm down, Lucky. I'm sure a plumber can—"

"Of all the dumb stunts! Why did you—"

"I was just trying to help," Angie sobbed. "I wanted you and Dr. Pam—" She twisted away from Pam's grasp and dashed from the kitchen, her cries heart wrenching as she ran through the dining room and up the stairs to her bedroom.

Arms extended and braced against the sink, Lucky was visibly trying to get himself back under control. His knuckles curled white over the edge of the counter and he drew a deep breath. "I blew it, didn't I?"

"You frightened her by yelling. She's a very insecure child."

"But candle wax? What a stupid—"

"She's only six, Lucky. It's easy to forget she's so young when she acts so grown-up so much of the time. But basically she's just a frightened child who has lost her parents. You can relate to that, can't you?"

He nodded and seemed to relax a little. "I gotta go apologize, don't I?"

She smiled at him. It took a great deal of courage to apologize to anyone, more so to a child when you're supposed to be an adult and know more than they do.

"What do I say?" he asked, his eyes beseeching her.

"I think if you just hold her, she'll understand. The words aren't important."

"I thought it would be easy. You know, being her dad for a while."

"I doubt very much that being a parent is ever easy. And face it, we're both brand-new at this. We're bound to make mistakes."

As he walked away heading for Angie's room, Pam realized she had included herself in the family equation. Odd how natural that had seemed. And troubling, too, because she doubted this fantasy Angie and Lucky appeared to be acting out could ever last.

A few minutes later, Lucky came back downstairs and announced they were all going shopping for more clothes for Angie.

"Sounds like you're trying to buy yourself back into her good graces," Pam teased.

He looked a little sheepish. "Well, they say when a woman gets down in the dumps a new outfit helps."

"I wouldn't know about that." She smiled at the way he was trying so hard to do the right thing. And probably spoiling Angie in the process. "A triple-chocolate fudge ice-cream cone always worked for me."

THE DECIBEL LEVEL reverberated through the mall as shoppers hurried to make their Christmas gift selections. Pam clung tightly to Angie's hand. In turn, the six-year-old hung on just as firmly to Lucky, making them appear to be a family of three on a shopping expedition.

They'd already purchased several new outfits for Angie, including a bright red dress for the holidays and patent leather shoes. Pam had watched wide-eyed as Lucky peeled off a couple of hundred-dollar bills from a fat stash in his money clip.

"Don't you believe in credit cards?" she asked. Lord, she counted herself fortunate when she had a twenty in her wallet.

"I've never known any store to turn away cash."

"But isn't it dangerous to carry so much money around? You could get mugged, or something."

He eyed her a moment with a sparkle of pure devilment. "Nobody's tried it yet. Maybe they know I fight dirty."

Pam clamped her mouth shut. Living on his own from such a young age, Lucky had learned to take care of himself without regard to any particular rules. He was a survivor, she realized. Probably with a very tough core and a great deal of inner strength—attributes that were hard not to admire.

She wondered if having been raised in a softer, kinder environment—however eccentric—had left her as strong.

"Hey, sport," Lucky said, pointing toward the center of a rotunda near the escalator. "There's Santa Claus. You wanta go tell him what you want for Christmas?"

She shook her head. "I don't believe in Santa."

"You don't?" How sad, Pam thought. Even in the worst of years, her parents had managed gifts from Santa for all three of their children.

"He never brings foster kids stuff. They move around too much."

Kneeling, Lucky linked his arm around the child's slender shoulders and gave her an awkward hug. "Yeah, I remember. But maybe this year will be different."

She looked at him with eyes far older and more solemn than her years warranted. "There's only one thing I really, truly want for Christmas, and I don't think Santa can help me get it."

Tears clogged Pam's throat. No child should have to carry burdens as heavy as those that rested on Angie's shoulders. Or those Lucky still carried with such aplomb.

IT WAS AFTER DINNER when Pam decided she needed to have a talk with Angie. She went upstairs and knocked on her door. The child had been so subdued since the fiasco with the candle wax, hardly even perking up during the shopping trip, Pam was concerned.

"May I come in?" she called.

"Sure."

As she opened the door, Angie scrambled up onto her full-size bed. The room was decorated in a Beatrix Potter motif, all rabbits and bright flowers, amazing Pam that a bachelor racehorse owner would have a perfect room waiting for a child just like Angie. Had he wanted children that much? she wondered. And, if so, why hadn't he married long ago?

"I thought I'd tuck you in for the night, if you'd like. I've been getting home so late every night, I haven't had the chance before. Lucky thought it would be all right."

"Is he still mad at me?"

"Of course not. Adults sometimes yell, but that doesn't mean they stay mad. Besides, he bought you a lot of new things this afternoon and he had a good time doing it."

Angie considered that for a moment, then said, "Okay." She squirmed under the covers and Pam sat down on the edge of the bed.

"Would you like me to read you a story?"

"Lucky usually reads me the sports page about horse racing. He don't gots any books for kids."

"Oh." Pam would make sure to remedy that situation as soon as possible. If she'd known, she would have bought some books at the mall that afternoon. "Would you like me to listen to your prayers?"

Angie scrunched up her nose. "I usually do that in private."

"I see." Apparently it was one thing to be board certified in pediatrics and something quite different to act as a surrogate mother, however temporarily. She brushed Angie's raggedy bangs back from her forehead. "Are you sure there isn't something you can tell us that will help us find your parents?"

"I think they're dead."

"What makes you think that?"

"'Cause I waited and waited for 'em to come get me, and nobody ever came."

"Where were you waiting?"

"In a bunch of places."

"In foster homes?"

Angie nodded. "Did you have any brothers or sisters there? If you did, you must miss them."

Angie scrunched up her face into what was surely meant to be a horrid face. "I don't want no brothers or sisters. I wanna be an *only* child."

"I thought if you could give us a clue—"

"That policeman at the hospital asked me all this stuff. I'm too little to remember."

Pam knew evasion when she heard it. "All right, honey. Maybe when you get a little bit older, you'll remember better." Or when she'd learned to trust and not fear another abandonment, she might be able to relate her past. A feeling which might take a very long time in coming.

She bent over and kissed Angie on the forehead. The child smelled sweet and clean from her bath, and Pam's heart filled with a surge of love. Tears stung at the back of her eyes in regret for all the children she would never bear, would never have a chance to love. "You sleep tight, little munchkin. I'll see you in the morning."

Her beeper—a device that was so much a part of her life, Pam often forgot she was wearing it—went off, startling her.

"What's that?" Angie asked, wide-eyed.

Pam checked the displayed numbers. "Looks like the hospital needs me. I may have to go into town, but Lucky will still be here if you need him."

"You aren't gonna stay home tonight and talk to Lucky?"

"Not if a sick child needs me at the hospital." When Angie's forehead pleated with a frown, Pam tucked the covers up under her chin. "How 'bout we all plan to go to church in the morning and you can wear your new dress. Would you like that?"

"Sure. I guess so."

"Good." She kissed her lightly on the cheek. "Sweet dreams."

Angie watched as Dr. Pam switched off the light and closed the bedroom door behind her.

She looked up into the darkened room and swallowed hard. "Are you there, Mister Saint Peter?"

"I'm still here, Angelica."

"I messed up today."

"You made a mistake. Most people do from time to time."

"Lucky was real mad at me."

"He apologized for yelling at you."

"Is he going to send me away?"

"I don't believe so, Angelica. I believe he is quite fond of you."

"Could you fix it so I don't mess up anymore?"

"That is something you will have to do for yourself, my child. We all have free choice. Even little children."

She sighed. That wasn't the answer she'd hoped for. She guessed she'd just have to try harder.

Chapter Six

There was a penalty for arriving late at church.

Pam felt two hundred pairs of eyes on her as she followed the usher down the aisle to the second row, right smack in front of the pulpit. Angie's hand was firmly tucked in hers, and Lucky trailed along in their wake.

Even during the sermon, the questioning gaze of the congregation prickled along her neck. She'd attended this church with Ted. He'd been an elder, an active member, and this had been only one of his many community involvements which had gained him the respect of the townspeople, as well as substantial donations to their clinic.

Now she was sitting in a pew with a man who was unknown to these people, a child sandwiched between them, and she suddenly wondered what the church's view was on horse racing and gambling. Particularly two-dollar bets that paid off big-time. She was afraid to even ask. Somehow she suspected there would be more eyebrows raised if they knew she was living in Lucky's house, however much it might be for a good cause and totally innocent—assuming one didn't assign too much weight to a wayward thought or two.

She sighed and waited impatiently for the service to conclude.

As the final hymn faded away, Pam thought she'd be able to make a clean getaway. But Eldyne Shoberg was too fast for her, trapping them in the aisle.

"Dear Pamela, what a sweet child you've brought to church with you." The minister's wife, a rotund self-appointed welcoming committee of one, bent over and squeezed Angie's cheek between her thumb and forefinger. "Aren't you the sweetest thing ever?"

"No, ma'am," Angie replied. She scrubbed her palm across her cheek as if she wanted to wipe away the affectionate pinch. "Sometimes I can be real bad."

"Oh, my..." Nonplussed, Eldyne shifted her attention to Lucky, extending her hand. "And you must be this sweet child's father."

"This is Lucky O'Toole," Pam interjected. "He was kind enough to offer a home to Angie when the hospital was unable to locate her family after she'd been in an accident. Lucky, this is Mrs. Shoberg, the minister's wife."

Lucky produced a smile warm enough to melt a two-ton iceberg. "Nice to meet you, Mrs. Shoberg. Please extend my compliments to your husband on his sermon this morning. He chose one of my favorite passages from the Bible and handled the intricacies of interpretation quite admirably."

Pam snapped him a surprised look. The sermon had gone totally over her head and would have put her to sleep if she hadn't been so concerned about what the members of the congregation were thinking.

"Aren't you a dear boy. I'll be sure to tell Bertrum you said so." Eldyne patted Lucky on the arm. "And I do hope you'll visit our little church again soon."

Lucky nodded noncommittally.

They'd hardly taken a step up the aisle away from Eldyne when Angie whispered sternly, "You're not s'posed to fib in church, Lucky."

"Only under special circumstances, sport." He winked. "You'll learn about that when you get bigger."

Angie didn't look convinced, and Pam wasn't either. But she was tickled. So much so she had to suppress a smile. Lucky had an uncanny way of striking a rare note on her funny bone, one that had far deeper repercussions that vibrated within her psyche.

Outside the church, Pam's escape was blocked by Roger Peltam, a big man with equally large political ambitions, at least as far as the town of Meadowbrook was concerned. He'd been on the city council for years and was the dominant force in the local Rotary Club.

He pecked her cheek with a kiss. "Good to see you in church, Dr. Pam." His bellowing voice boomed so loudly that all of the remaining churchgoers milling around the grassy square were included in the conversation. "We still miss ol' Ted, but it's good you're getting out and about."

Pam responded with an inadequate, "Thank you."

He extended his hand to Lucky. "Don't believe I've had the pleasure."

As Lucky introduced himself, he felt an unexpected rush of antagonism. Who was this guy? he wondered. A rival? Somebody Pam wanted him to meet so she could prove the orphan kid who'd made it big still didn't measure up? He struggled to suppress old insecurities that had dogged him until only recently.

Peltam pumped his hand a little longer than necessary. "Say now, you're the fellow who took a swipe with your car at our nativity scene, aren't you?"

"I'm afraid so," Lucky agreed tautly.

"Well, I've been talkin' to the ol' boys in the Rotary. We think we can raise enough money to replace the crèche and all those plaster statues. Course, it may be next year before we—"

"It's been taken care of."

Roger's eyes narrowed. "Did the Kiwanis beat us to it? Those guys—and gals, too, of course—are quick to pick up on the good projects. Real quick."

"I've taken care of things myself," Lucky announced, pleased he could show up this blustering hotshot. "The supplies should be here this week and the construction crew will have things back together by church service on Sunday."

"That a fact?" Peltam actually looked disappointed that he'd been displaced as the hero for the day. "Well now, you sure you're not letting the Kiwanis take all the credit? Maybe you could let the Rotary—"

"I'm not much of a joiner, Roger. If you don't mind, I'll do this on my own."

Pam wasn't quite sure what to make of that exchange, and Lucky's uncharacteristic animosity, but Roger said his goodbyes then drifted off to pursue his politics with someone else.

"Well, did I pass the test?" Lucky asked as they headed for his beat-up farm truck that he had insisted they come in. Angie had run ahead.

Pam's head swiveled left. "I beg your pardon?"

"Did you think I wouldn't clean up good enough to go to church with you?"

"That's not so." In fact, he looked quite devastating in his dark blue suit, white shirt and striking silk tie that managed to bring out the brilliant sapphire color of his eyes.

"But you were thinking I wouldn't quite measure up to your friends, weren't you?"

"I thought nothing of the sort. But I was surprised you knew so much about Biblical references," she admitted.

"Trust me, the nuns at the orphanage drilled a lot of stuff into my head. Some of which may have even stuck. But I didn't have a clue as to what the preacher was talking about this morning. And neither did you."

"Then you—"

"*Fibbed,* as Angie puts it. But I didn't lie about not being a joiner. The Association of Racehorse Owners gets my annual dues, and I'm involved with the Track Employees Welfare Foundation, but that's it. I've been on my own since I was fourteen. There haven't been many who have given me a leg up, except Rafael. You can introduce me to whoever you want, but I'm not about to fawn all over some guy who thinks the sun rises and sets on mumbo jumbo or a secret handshake."

"I certainly didn't mean to suggest—"

"Why did I get the feeling in church that what those people think is important to you? Could it be you're a small-town snob, Pam?"

She blanched, hoping he wasn't right. And suspecting he might have touched on an unwelcome truth. As a physician, having the community's respect was crucial to her.

"You shouldn't have antagonized Roger, and I don't dare," she said defensively. "The Rotary makes a substantial annual contribution to the clinic."

"Which your husband arranged."

"Yes. He was very good at—"

"You want to fit in with the group so much you've turned yourself into a peg that will fit into whatever mold they want. I'm not about to do that for you or anybody else."

They'd reached the truck and he spun her around, trapping her between the vehicle and his hard body. "Frankly, sweetheart, I prefer my women with a few rough edges that no amount of pressure can wear down. In a horse, it's called spirit."

"I'm not—" Myriad emotions assaulted Pam. Her whole body tightened with sexual awareness. He was standing too close, his impact far too masculine for anything but an intimate response. A *feminine* response, right here in the church parking lot. Outrageous. Impossible. And totally irresistible. "I'm not..." she swallowed hard "...a horse."

"Yeah," he drawled, eyeing her with unnerving speculation. "I've noticed. And it irritates the hell out of me."

"It *irritates?*" she exploded.

"I think I'd be better off not wanting you."

"The feeling is mutual, I assure you."

"That you want me? Or that you don't like the idea of wanting me?"

"Both."

He grinned. "Now we're getting somewhere."

"I didn't mean—"

"I think you did. In fact, when you get uppity like this, it makes me want you more than I've ever wanted any woman in my life."

"That's *your* problem." If she could have backed away, she would have. Or if a scream would have solved the problem, she would have done that. But the fact was, she found Lucky O'Toole absolutely fascinating, unlike any man she'd ever known. And as irritating as a burrowing tick. He'd wrapped the minister's wife around his little finger, and put the pompous Rotary president in his place. Ever since she'd met Lucky, she'd been torn between laughter and fury. It was a most disconcerting experience. And thoroughly exhilarating.

"Could we discuss this in a more private setting?" she pleaded.

"Are you saying you're interested in pursuing the logical outcome if we both want each other so darn much?"

"I'm suggesting we have a six-year-old child in the audience, along with half the congregation of Meadowbrook Church. This isn't the time or place to make any rash decisions."

A triumphant smile creased his cheeks. "I can deal with that."

Pam wasn't at all sure she would fare as well. She'd all but agreed she was going to go to bed with him— eventually. And that's not at all what she'd meant.

He opened the truck door and Angie scrambled into the cab. "Can we go have ice cream now?" she asked.

"Lunch first," Lucky replied. "Then we'll all get triple-chocolate-fudge double-dippers."

Pam swallowed back a smile. Though she wasn't in the least depressed, she could always handle a little extra chocolate just in case. And she was inordinately pleased Lucky had remembered her favorite flavor.

Trying to follow Angie into the truck, her mood shifted quickly and she mentally cursed the wardrobe choice she'd made for herself that morning. Stiletto heels and a pencil-straight skirt might give her a break from her workday attire but were all wrong for easy access to the cab of a truck. She wished now she had insisted they bring her car this morning. But Lucky and Angie had already been in the truck with the motor running when she'd come out of the house. She'd been late, she suspected, because she'd been primping too much for his benefit.

Lucky's hands closed around her waist and his lips moved down near her ear. "Sweetheart, you've got great legs. But if you hike up your skirt far enough to get into the truck, what happens next will count as one of the world's most embarrassing moments. I hate to see a man's zipper burst. Particularly in a church parking lot." In a breath-taking moment, he lifted her and placed her on the seat.

She gasped and caught his forearms to steady herself, feeling the steely strength that hid beneath his suit jacket.

The beeper in Pam's purse went off.

It took her three full heartbeats before she could drag her gaze away from Lucky to check who was trying to reach her.

"The hospital," she said in a daze. Never before had she been plagued by so many erotic thoughts. *Inappropriate* thoughts that were totally out of character.

"Aren't there any other pediatricians in town?" he grumbled, releasing his grip on her.

"It's my on-call weekend."

"I thought we were gonna have ice cream," Angie complained.

"Why don't you drop me off at the hospital," Pam suggested to Lucky, "then you two can go on—"

"Will it take you long?"

"I won't know till I get there."

"Tell you what." He stepped back to close the door. "Angie and I will stick around and see how it goes. Maybe there's still a chance we can have lunch together."

SHE'D MISSED both lunch and dinner before she had a chance to see Lucky again. She tossed her purse on a stand in the entry hall and headed for the TV room. Angie had long since gone to bed and Pam curled herself into her favorite corner of Lucky's couch, sighing with relief to be home. Her back ached; her feet were swollen two sizes larger than normal. So much for impressing her patients—or Lucky—with stiletto heels.

"Long day?" he queried, raising his brows.

"Sundays can be the pits. Patients can't locate their own doctors, so they show up at emergency. I've never understood why ear infections and bronchitis are so virulent on weekends. And tonight—" A silent sob caught in her throat. She didn't want to think about her last little patient.

"Hey, what happened?" Sympathetically, he sat down beside her.

"Just one of those...horrible things."

"You want to tell me about it?"

She shouldn't. She certainly didn't want to break down. But sometimes it hurt too much to keep inside all she'd seen and felt. "There was a little boy about five years old. His mother...held the child's hand over the flame of hot stove."

"Why the hell did she do that?"

"Because she thought he'd been touching himself..." Pam's voice hitched again, her control slipping. "She wanted to punish him." The tears that had threatened since the police had brought the child into emergency welled up. As hard as she tried, she couldn't stop them. They poured down her cheeks like a dam had been broken. She bit her lower lip, and still the tears flowed.

Lucky gathered her into his arms. "Shh, sweetheart, it's okay to cry."

Shaking her head, she sobbed, "I'm supposed to be objective. I'm a doctor."

"Yeah, but you don't have to be a tough guy all the time. Not around me."

"It was so awful, Lucky. It was all I could do not to find the woman and kill her myself. How could any mother do that to..." The words lodged in her throat and stuck there.

Lucky held her while she soaked his shirt with her tears. She couldn't remember the last time she'd let go like this, but it felt good to have a shoulder to cry on. A strong, sympathetic shoulder that didn't give her professional platitudes like Ted used to but simply let her have a good cry. Sometimes that's exactly what a woman needed.

Eventually the tears ran their course and Pam drew a hiccupy breath. "I've ruined your shirt."

"It was worth it. Now I know for sure how much you care about your patients, even when you try to hide behind your stethoscope."

She raised her head to gaze at him. "You may be giving me more credit than I deserve."

"I don't think so." He ran his knuckles down her damp cheek. "I may not be able to help that kid you saw this evening, but I think I've got something that will lift your spirits."

"Oh? What's that?"

"You'll see." Deftly, he slipped away from her and headed for the kitchen.

Pam used his absence to try to gather herself, wiping her eyes with the back of her hand and running her fingers through her hair to restore some semblance of order.

A few minutes later, he returned from the kitchen with a bowl heaped with double-double chocolate to-die-for ice cream. Smiling at the perfect antidote to a stressful day, Pam dipped the spoon he'd provided into the ice cream, savored the flavor and sighed.

"You, sir, are a miracle worker. It's possible I may even survive until the morrow."

"I certainly hope so." He settled down next to her on the couch again. "I'm getting kinda used to having you around."

An unfamiliar warmth flooded through her body, weighting her limbs. "I'm not sure I'm even earning my keep—the money you've pledged to the clinic."

"You think Angie is the only reason I'm glad you're here?"

"Well, I . . . that is—"

His slow, sensuous smile halted her words. "Here, let me try some of my famous sleight of hand." Lifting her legs, he stretched them out across his lap and began to knead her tired feet.

"Heaven," she groaned, closing her eyes. "Wherever did you learn to do that?" The feelings he conjured were exquisite, both relaxing and exhilarating at the same time, particularly after such an emotionally draining day.

"I had a girlfriend once who worked as a waitress."

"And she let you get away?"

He chuckled, his hands soothing over the arch of her foot, feeling the delicate structure of her bones. He liked pampering a woman. And sensed Pam hadn't had much of that in her life. She wasn't tough. She was soft, inside and out, and for some reason hated to let anyone see the truth. Even though he wasn't a rocket scientist, he'd known that all along. "Maybe she wasn't interested in a man with a foot fetish."

Pam's big, brown eyes opened slowly. "Foolish girl." She took a bite of ice cream, then ran her tongue along the contour of her lips.

Lucky's groin muscles tightened. He knew exactly how her lips would taste—sweet and slick with the flavor of chocolate mixing with her own special essence.

Sliding his hand up to her calf, he massaged her lightly. Her stockings made her legs smooth as silk, but he imagined her flesh would be even more tempting to the touch.

She looked tired, with lines of stress around her full lips and etching the corners of her red-rimmed eyes. He wished he could ease the rest of her tension. And his, too, he realized, knowing *his* stress had nothing to do with overwork or an emotional day.

"Oh, I don't know," he said, masking his real feelings as he responded to her flattering comment. "We were both about eighteen at the time and had a lot of roads yet to travel."

"You've never married?"

"Nope." Though the errant thought had entered his mind a lot lately—about how much he liked the lingering scent of a woman in his house, her quick blush when she read his sexual innuendos, and how having her around on a permanent basis wouldn't be all bad.

"Why not?" Pam glanced away, embarrassed. "I'm sorry. I'm being nosy."

"It's okay. The answer is simple enough. I've never met a woman I wanted to spend the rest of my life with."

She ate the remaining few bites of ice cream in silence, acutely aware of the warmth generated by Lucky's palm on her leg, contrasting with the cold chocolate melting in her mouth. Somewhere in another part of the house she heard a noise. Something soft, almost furtive. Angie getting up? The wind rattling a window? It didn't matter. If any crisis was about to happen, it was right here. With Lucky. And the thoroughly arousing way he was caressing her leg. He was a man skillful at seduction, she realized dimly, even as she continued to enjoy the sensation in spite of her best intentions not to let this sort of thing happen between them. Clearly her crying jag had weakened her resolve.

"So what have you decided, Doc?" he questioned, his voice rough, his hand edging upward.

Her heated response arrowed toward her nether regions. "About what?"

"About trying another experiment. Maybe upstairs, your bedroom or mine. Whichever you prefer."

Her nerves jumped and tangled together, and she tried to withdraw her legs. He didn't release her. "I don't think that's wise."

"See, the problem is, I can't seem to get you out of my head."

She couldn't stop thinking about Lucky, either. But she wasn't about to admit that. "O'Toole, I don't jump into an affair with any man whom I happen to meet."

"You're selective. I like that. I'm kinda picky myself."

"That sounded like a backhanded compliment."

"I'm not real good at poetry and roses. I suppose your husband was?"

"As a matter of fact, yes." At least Ted had been quite attentive during their courtship. He'd always known what to say, picked the perfect gift for a special occasion. After that... Well, a lot of married couples shift into a lower gear, and it didn't matter that she'd missed some of the extra attention, the specialness they'd once had. After all, they'd both been busy with the clinic. It was of no significance that with Lucky she felt an excitement, an undiagnosable thrill, that she couldn't ever remember experiencing with Ted. Not even in the early days of their courtship. Perhaps she had simply forgotten.

"Chalk it up to my disadvantaged youth," Lucky continued. "My tastes are pretty basic—in both women and sex."

She squirmed away from his grasp. "Primitive seems a more apt description." And she seemed to be responding in the same elemental way.

He gave her wicked, teasing look. "I love it when you talk dirty to me, Doc. Really gets my juices going."

"That wasn't—" Exasperated as much by her own roiling emotions as by Lucky's determined onslaught of sexual innuendo, Pam rose in as much of a huff as she could manage, considering a part of her would have chosen to accept his invitation to pick a bedroom. "Unlike some people I know, I've got to go to work tomorrow. Thank you for the ice cream and the foot massage. And the shoulder to cry on."

"You're welcome. Anytime."

Unwilling to meet his gaze—which she was sure would accuse her of being a coward—she fled the room. She searched for her purse where she thought she had left it in the entry hall, but with no success. She wasn't about to ask Lucky for help. The fact was, one more suggestive comment from him and she'd turn totally witless. *Whose* bedroom would no longer be an issue. She'd ravish him right where he stood.

Knowing her telephone service could reach her by phone if they didn't get an answer on her missing beeper, Pam headed upstairs determined to get a good night's sleep. Alone.

IN SPITE OF a cloud-covered sky, Pam woke early. Awareness prickled along the back of her neck. Something was wrong.

She rolled over to check the clock. The digital numbers blinked twelve o'clock over and over again. Sometime during the night the power had been lost, not an unusual phenomenon in rural Meadowbrook.

Easing her legs over the edge of the bed, she reached for the phone to check the time. The squalling dial tone announcing an instrument off the hook greeted her. Wincing at the sharp sound, she pulled on a robe and went in search of the offending phone. She found it in Lucky's downstairs office.

Puzzled, and remembering that her beeper was missing, she waited a moment after she hung up, then dialed her phone service.

"Hi, Marcy, it's Dr. Pam."

"Good morning, doctor," the operator said cheerily. "We've been trying to reach you all night."

"You have?"

"Robyn Merced took a turn for the worse last night. Her parents reported temperatures up to 105 degrees, loss of consciousness—"

"My God—" Robyn was only a baby—six months old with a viral infection.

"When I couldn't reach you, they decided to take her in to Escondido, to the Tri-Cities Hospital. That was probably about midnight."

Pam's fingers closed tightly around the phone. "You tried my beeper?"

"Sure. Then I tried the number you'd given me. But I got a busy signal. I rang several times. Sorry."

"That's all right, Marcy. It was my fault. I'll check on Robyn right away."

It took her only a moment to dial Tri-Cities Hospital, seconds more to reach the nursing station on the pediatric floor. To her great relief, the nurse reported Robyn's temperature had responded to the on-call physician's treatment, and the child was resting comfortably.

Thanking the nurse, Pam cradled the phone.

Now, she thought grimly, she was going to find out why her beeper was missing and why the phone had been off the hook all night.

Chapter Seven

"I didn't mean for anybody to get hurt." Sitting at the kitchen table, Angie hung her head and fiddled with the big yellow flower on the oversize T-shirt she wore as a nightgown.

Pam knelt in front of her. "Then why did you hide my beeper and take the phone off the hook?"

She lifted her narrow shoulders in an awkward shrug.

"Angelica," Pam said sternly. "A little child—a baby—could have died because of what you did. I want to know why."

Lucky's hand closed over Pam's shoulder, silently reminding her to remain calm. She had gone to him first thing this morning, thinking that he might have accidentally forgotten to hang up the phone—or perhaps forgotten on purpose so the provocative scene in the TV room last night could have played itself out into a full-blown seduction scene. But he'd denied that was the case and her suspicions had been unwarranted. She had misjudged him, possibly because there'd been a fair amount of wishful thinking on her part.

In contrast, Angie had readily admitted her guilt.

The child lifted her gaze; her eyes were filled with billowing tears. Her chin wobbled. "I'm sorry."

"I understand that, but it doesn't excuse what you did."

"It would be better if you tell us what's going on, sport," Lucky encouraged.

Angie blinked and a single tear trickled down her cheek. "I heard you come in last night, Dr. Pam, and then I heard you 'n Lucky talkin' and stuff." She drew a shaky breath. "I didn't want you to go back to the hospital. I wanted you to stay here with Lucky."

Matchmaking again. Pam wondered why it was so terribly important to a six-year-old that she and Lucky become a couple. The child's interest appeared to specifically focus on just the two of them, when any two caring parents should have been able to meet Angie's need for love.

Resting her hands lightly on Angie's thighs, Pam said, "I want you to promise me you'll never, *ever* do that again. My patients have to be able to reach me."

"I promise." She looked at Pam solemnly. "Are you going to spank me?"

"No, I don't spank children, honey. But maybe you can think of a punishment that would help you appreciate what you did was very wrong."

"I have to decide my pun'ment for myself?"

"I think you're big enough to do that."

Her forehead furrowed. "That's hard."

Pam waited patiently for Angie's decision. Lucky's hand was comforting on her shoulder, his fingers kneading lightly as he offered quiet support. Idly she wondered how single parents ever managed their children when they had to provide all the loving and dish out the discipline, too. Then Pam realized she shouldn't be thinking of parenthood at all. Hers was a temporary situation—a few weeks or months of pretending to be Angie's mother, then Lucky would no longer need her once he was officially appointed her guardian. Assuming the child's real family hadn't yet been located.

"I guess..." Angie hesitated, lifting her chin in a show of heart-breaking bravery. "It'd be real bad if I didn't get to go visit Hot Diggity and the other horses for a whole day."

"That would be rough," Lucky agreed.

Pam swallowed down the lump that filled her throat. "I think that's a perfect penalty for a little girl who loves horses as much as you do. You're very wise to have thought of it." She smoothed Angie's uneven bangs away from her forehead, imagining the child would have happily settled for an old-fashioned spanking instead of the far harsher punishment she'd selected for herself. Lord, being a mom, even for a little while, was harder than she had thought. "Maybe sometime later this week we can find something special we can all do together."

Angie brightened at the possibility. "We can?"

"I know the perfect thing," Lucky announced.

Hand on the table, Pam levered herself to her feet and Lucky scooped Angie up into his arms, giving her a quick hug, a perfect way to let the child know she was still loved.

"Sweet Sigh is running at Hollywood Park on Wednesday—her first race at a mile and an eighth," Lucky said. "We could drive up there and make a day of it. You know, lunch in the clubhouse. First post is at twelve-thirty."

"Oh, wow! Could we, Dr. Pam? Could we?"

"I don't know," Pam hedged. "I usually work Wednesday mornings."

"So take a day off, Doc. If you don't need some rest and relaxation, you can bet Irma Sue does."

"Well, I guess it would be all right, if I can rearrange my schedule..." She waited to be swept with the feeling of contrition at the mere thought of playing hooky, but it didn't come. Instead, a pleasurable smile curled her lips. She couldn't think of anything she'd enjoy more than spending a day with Lucky and Angie. "Just this once."

Still in Lucky's arms, Angie lunged toward Pam, hugged her and kissed her hard on the cheek. "Thank you, Dr. Pam. I won't ever, *ever* hide your beeper again. I promise."

Pam laughed and felt as if a six-year-old child with bright blue eyes and a breathtaking smile had just stolen a piece of her heart. She knew she'd never quite be the same again.

Even more troubling, Lucky's matching smile hinted at being similarly life changing.

Squirming out of Lucky's arms, her mood much improved, Angie raced out of the kitchen and upstairs to get dressed for breakfast.

Lucky shook his head. "I was wrong. You're one tough cookie, Pamela Jones. Remind me not to cross swords with you anytime soon. Making the poor kid pick her own poison—that's downright underhanded. But admirable," he conceded with an understanding smile.

"I don't know." Pam poured a cup of coffee and questioned him with her eyes to see if he'd like a cup, too.

"Sure," he said. "Thanks."

"My clever disciplining scheme may have backfired. I feel hugely guilty right about now. She loves your horses so much, *I'm* going to be miserable all day knowing she can't be out there with them."

"Yeah, I know how you feel. I was thinking I'd get her a horse for Christmas. I'd guess that's what she has been talking about, the one thing she wants more than anything else that Santa Claus couldn't give her. Rafael is checking around to see if he can find a gentle mare for her."

"Oh, Lucky, I'm not sure that's a good idea. What if her parents—"

"Relax, Doc. If they were going to show up, they would have by now."

"Maybe. The police chief is still checking."

He cocked his head. "Have you always been so darn levelheaded?"

"Why, I . . . Yes, I guess I have."

"That's too bad."

"It's hardly something I need to be ashamed of."

Lifting his hip, he settled it on the corner of the table. If the man would learn to button up his shirt, maybe Pam could learn to deal with him better. Of course, she'd burst into his bedroom this morning to accuse him of stealing her beeper, only to discover he slept naked except for his jockey shorts—shorts that clung to every ridge and impressive bulge of his pelvis. Even now she kept thinking how she'd like to run her fingertips through the dark hair that swirled across his chest and feel the underlying muscles, and how the nest of his manhood would be an even more tempting destination for her exploration. Those were hardly appropriate thoughts first thing in the morning when she should be on her way to the office. Nor were they images she remembered considering with Ted. Lucky, it seemed, had a far different effect on her than had her husband. Until now, she never would have suspected she had a mind that could fill with such erotic possibilities.

Oddly, she wondered if she'd missed something in her relationship with Ted.

"So, who convinced you that you weren't allowed to have any fun?" Lucky asked, breaking into her thoughts.

"I have fun."

"Yeah, right."

"Some people are more responsible than others," she said defensively. "It's in their nature."

"And sometimes people are forced to be responsible when down deep they want to cut loose a little."

She narrowed her gaze. "My parents believed in cutting loose a *lot*, so much so there were times when we didn't have enough to eat. More than once I had to lie to our landlord, swearing my parents weren't at home when they were hiding because they couldn't pay the rent." The memory of humiliation still tasted bitter in her mouth. She slid a piece of bread in the toaster and jammed down the lever hard. "I'd say being *responsible* was a virtue."

"How old were you?" he asked softly.

"I don't know. Ten or eleven, I suppose." Her hand shook as she retrieved the butter from the refrigerator. "My mother was a sometime stunt woman in Hollywood. She still is, for that matter. She'd taken a bad fall that year and broke her leg. I was trying to take care of her, and my brother and sister. Mom was out of commission and Dad couldn't find any work. That's when I decided . . . I decided I'd be a doctor and then if Mom hurt herself again I'd be able…" Lord, she hated those memories, her dark fear that her mother would be so badly hurt, like Humpty Dumpty, nobody would be able to put her back together again.

Cupping Pam's chin, Lucky skimmed his thumb across her cheek, wiping away a tear she hadn't realized she'd shed.

Embarrassment heated her face. "I feel so foolish. It seems like I'm always crying around you. That's not like me. It really isn't."

"Shh, darlin'. I understand. You shouldn't have tried to take the whole world on your shoulders. Nobody is that strong. And you weren't much bigger than Angie is."

"But someone had to look after—"

"My personal prescription, Doc, is to take a big dose of fun. All you can get. We'll start with a megadose Wednesday at the racetrack."

"I've never been to the races."

His eyebrows shot up in total disbelief. "You haven't?"

"Not even once."

"You, sweetheart, are in for the biggest treat of your life."

He lowered his head and soundly kissed her. For a moment Pam wasn't sure if the treat he had in mind was a day at the races or his thoroughly titillating kiss. Then, for some reason, it didn't matter one way or the other. She was simply caught up in the persuasive movements of his lips and the twirling temptation of his tongue.

FOR A LONG TIME after Pam left for her office, Lucky prowled the house. He hadn't meant to kiss her. But she'd looked so damn vulnerable, he couldn't help himself. And then he'd had a helluva time not tossing her over his shoulder and hauling her upstairs to his bedroom where he could make love to her for the rest of the morning.

Never in his life had he been quite so out of control when it came to a woman. *Poleaxed* was beginning to sound like a serious understatement.

Eventually he wandered outside. Angie was hard at work at the kitchen table with glue, scissors and colored paper making something very secretive. Probably a Christmas decoration, he imagined. In fact, it occurred to him they ought to get a Christmas tree pretty soon. If Angie's parents did show up...

Well, he didn't have much faith they'd even remember there was a holiday coming.

As he entered the horse barn, Rafael looked at him curiously but remained silent. The old man was as close to a father as Lucky had ever had. He'd shown him the ropes when he was so wet behind the ears he hadn't even known how to wield a shovel and broom. With Rafael's tutoring, he'd learned in a hurry, and every muscle in his body still remembered the lessons.

Picking up a handful of oats from a feed sack, Lucky offered the grain to Hot Tops, a thoroughbred he kept at stud. The horse nibbled lightly at his palm.

"You seem restless, my son," Rafael said.

"A little," Lucky conceded.

"Perhaps that means it is time for you to fill up all those bedrooms you have in that big house of yours."

"With what?" In spite of his bravado, Lucky wasn't sure how long he'd be able to keep Angie. And Pam was likely to bolt at any moment.

"With babies, of course." Rafael leaned on his rake. "She would be a good mother, would she not?"

"Yeah. Terrific."

"Then there is some other problem?"

"She's a doctor, Rafael. She's probably got degrees in stuff I can't even pronounce."

"I think it is not so important what a woman has tacked on after her name, only what is in her heart."

"I suppose." The problem was, Lucky didn't have a clue as to what was going on in Pam's head, much less her heart. He only knew she wasn't the kind of woman who would settle for a one-night stand. And he wasn't that kind of guy, either. Not anymore. Still, what the hell did he know about commitment? Except for Rafael, he'd never had much of a role model.

Somewhere in his gut, he felt that Pam deserved better.

PAM HURRIED ACROSS the hospital lobby. Lucky was waiting for her outside and her last minute instructions to the nurses upstairs had taken longer than she had expected.

Police Chief Coleman was striding toward her. "Morning, Dr. Pam. You look downright spiffy today." His broad smile lifted his carefully groomed mustache.

She flushed and thanked him. Not knowing quite what the appropriate attire might be for the races, she'd chosen a print dress with a full skirt and shoes that would be comfortable for walking, then added simple hoop earrings. If anything, she might look a little too summery or frivolous, but there was no time to change her mind now. "Any word on Angie's parents yet?" she asked as she crossed paths with the chief.

"Not yet. The FBI should be getting back to us anytime now. Unless it's a criminal case, they're not known for their speedy responses."

Pam had gathered as much, and somewhere in her heart she'd begun to hope Angie's parents would never be found. Which wasn't fair to the child, but Pam had come to the conclusion that Angie would be far better off with Lucky than a family that had apparently abandoned her.

Once Pam stepped out of the hospital, all thoughts of Angie and the child's problems fled. Instead, what she felt was a burst of unadulterated pleasure to find Lucky standing by his car, smiling his most contagious smile and looking as handsome as any man she had ever seen. A kelly green ascot with a four-leaf clover design set off his light blue blazer and emphasized the striking color of his eyes; his legs were long and lean above spotless white loafers. Returning his smile, she noted a lock of windblown hair had drifted down over his forehead, and she had to repress the urge to finger-comb it back into place.

"You ready to go?" he asked, opening the passenger door.

Oh, yes, she was *ready*—ready for things she shouldn't be wanting, or even be thinking about.

She slid into the front seat of the Ferrari and the leather surrounded her in a soft embrace. She almost sighed at the sheer decadent feeling of such opulence and the unexpectedly wicked thought that Lucky's hands would feel equally good caressing her.

"Sorry. I had to see a couple of patients this morning," she said as Lucky settled behind the steering wheel. "I know you wanted to leave first thing."

"No problem. I sent Angie off with Rafael and José. She's tickled pink to get to spend more time with the horses, and I get a chance to show off my car." He switched on the ignition and the engine hummed with restrained power.

"It doesn't look any worse for wear after the accident." In fact, the glossy black shine and sleek lines made the car look as if it were speeding when it was sitting in the parking lot. Quite a contrast to her gothic gray conservative sedan, which appeared to be made from the same cookie-cutter mold as every other car on the road.

With a flick of his wrist, he shifted and they sped out onto the street. "The paint shop did a good job smoothing out the scratches. You've gotta look real close to see that there's ever been a nick."

Pam adjusted the scarf she'd brought along in anticipation of a top-down ride. Only in Southern California in December, she mused with a smile.

Within minutes, he had accelerated onto the freeway, heading north toward Los Angeles. He glanced in her direction, a grin creasing his cheeks. "This is great, huh?"

She nodded her approval. He was like an eager little boy who'd just gotten his toy—his very *expensive* toy—back in one piece, and he couldn't wait to see if all the parts were still working.

Riding so low to the ground with the wind blowing in her face, the sense of speed was exhilarating. She could understand how a person could become addicted to the feeling. Just as she was growing increasingly hooked on being with Lucky. In spite of her best efforts to deny the truth, he had an uncanny way of making her feel light-hearted and extraordinarily feminine.

She leaned back and let these new sensations overtake her. At some intuitive level, she knew it was a miracle she felt so suddenly and fully alive. And the miracle worker was an intriguing man named Lucky O'Toole.

ANGIE SPOTTED THEM as they walked into the grandstand. She escaped from Rafael and raced up the aisle, launching herself into Lucky's arms.

Pam smiled indulgently. The two of them were quite a pair.

"I gots to see *all* the horses, Lucky," Angie announced in a high-pitched voice. "One of 'em was swimmin' in a *big* swimmin' pool. And there were some walkin' 'round and 'round on this funny merry-go-round." She drew a quick breath and shot a mischievous grin in Pam's direction. "Rafael said if I was bad, he'd hook me up to that thing and I'd go 'round and 'round forever. But he didn't mean it.''

"I'm sure he didn't," Pam conceded with a smile. Lucky and Angie were so easy about sharing their affection, while she tended to hold back. But maybe among the three of them, at least one person needed to keep her feet firmly planted on solid ground. That had always been Pam's role, and it would be hard to change at this late date, however buoyant Lucky made her feel.

"So how did Sweet Sigh look to you?" Lucky asked Angie.

"José says she's gonna win. It's a sure thing. Are you gonna bet on her, Lucky?"

"Maybe a few dollars. Wouldn't want to miss a sure thing."

Pam winced. She really didn't believe in gambling, but then . . . "What race is she running in?"

"The third."

"I brought along a little extra money—"

"What?" His eyebrows raised. "The world's most conservative doc is planning to place a bet?"

"I won't exactly be risking the rent money."

Laughing, he looped his free arm around her shoulders, drawing her into the circle of his affection. "A race is a lot more fun if you've got a few dollars riding on the outcome."

Pam wondered how much he'd have riding. A potential Derby winner had to be worth thousands. If the filly fell or was bumped . . .

Pam stopped herself. For today, she wasn't going to take on any extra worries. It was simply enough to enjoy the excitement of the milling crowds and the tote board racking up the ever-changing odds. And being with Lucky.

They were eating lunch in the clubhouse when the horses were called to the gate for the first race.

Angie sat up on her knees and dug into her pocket, producing two one-dollar bills and some change that she plunked down across the table in front of Lucky. "I want to make a bet," she said.

"Where'd you get the money?" he asked.

"It's what I won from you at gin rummy."

"Oh. Okay, who do you want to bet on?"

"Lucky, isn't there a law about having to be an adult before you can bet?" Pam questioned. She nudged him with her elbow.

He shrugged. "You know you could lose it all, don't you, sport?"

"But I won't. José said he gots a tip that can't fail."

Pam winced. No good ever came from easy money.

"If you're sure," Lucky said. "But I'm warning you, you're taking a risk. There's no handicapper in the world who makes all of his bets. And that includes me."

Angie jutted her chin up at a stubborn angle. "I wanna bet on Little Teaser."

Lucky checked the tote board. "Oh, wow, that's a twenty-to-one shot. That's not a good bet, sport. A sucker bet." When Angie didn't budge, he signaled the waiter over, took two dollars from Angie's stash and sent the young man on his way. There were only a few coins left on the table.

With a final admonishing glare, Pam looked away, out across the racecourse. Hollywood Park was larger than she had anticipated and far lovelier. The grassy infield was a bright green—even in the dead of winter—and the attractive sculpted pond in the middle was populated with geese and migrating ducks. None of that meant she approved of Lucky encouraging a six-year-old to gamble. On the other hand, losing her money might be a lesson Angie would long remember.

The horses paraded past the grandstand, the jockeys' silks bright exclamation points against the burnt sienna of the track. The tension in the clubhouse mounted, and Pam caught the excitement. Adrenaline pushed her heart rate up a notch. Vaguely, she was aware of the waiter returning with the betting ticket and handing it to Lucky. But she kept her eyes on the horses making their way into the starting gates.

They were off!

It was all Pam could do to stay in her seat. The horses were magnificent creatures thundering toward the first turn. So powerful they were absolutely breathtaking.

A strong, callused hand covered hers.

"Pretty exciting, uh?" Lucky asked. His voice was husky, teasing with its warmth against her ear.

"Yes . . . I didn't know."

He handed her a pair of field glasses and she raised them to her eyes. To her surprise, on the far side of the track Little Teaser was running in second place and driving hard. "Come on, Teaser!" she shouted.

Angie echoed the cry.

Oh, shoot! There was no way she could sit still when Angie's bet was at stake.

Before she knew what she was doing, Pam was on her feet, shouting and cheering as if her entire bank account were riding on Little Teaser. The bay challenged the leader, then fell back, only to try again—*teasing* the fans. For a full thirty seconds, pandemonium reigned in the clubhouse. Then the lead horses charged past the finish line, Little Teaser winning by a nose.

"Oh my goodness!" Laughing, Pam gasped for breath and her knees went rubbery. She settled weakly back into her chair.

"I win! I win!" Angie shouted jubilantly.

"That you do, sport. Forty bucks."

The child's eyes widened.

A cold sense of dread knotted in Pam's stomach. This was not a good lesson for a child to learn.

"Can I bet all that on the next race?" Angie asked.

"You can if you want," Lucky explained. "If you win again, it's a daily double. But I wouldn't count on it."

"José says—"

Pam decided José ought to be horsewhipped.

"—Catch-22 is gonna win."

Lucky signaled the waiter again.

Under her breath, Pam whispered, "You can't let her do this. Forty dollars is a huge amount of money for a—"

"Maybe she'll be lucky," he said, winking. "I was."

Pam fumed. People made their own luck through hard work. That's what she believed. Clearly she and Lucky had far different views of what contributed to success.

The wait for the next race was interminable. When it began, Pam felt nothing but dread. Suddenly too much rode on the outcome. The risk was too great for a child who had already suffered so much in her young life.

Chapter Eight

She'd lost. The *whole* forty dollars. More money than she'd ever had in her entire life.

Angie leaned against the railing in the grandstand and glowered up at the pretty blue sky.

"You could have helped a little, if you'd wanted to," she said accusingly.

We have discussed this before, Angelica. Greed is not a becoming attribute among humans.

"I was gonna use the money to buy Lucky and Dr. Pam a real nice present for Christmas."

I understand that. But I think they will be happy if you give them something that comes from your heart. It does not have to cost a great deal of money.

She sighed. Saint Peter could be pretty darn hard to get along with sometimes.

"Hey, sport." Lucky lifted Angie, gave her a squeeze, then sat her on top of the railing in front of their grandstand seats. It always made her feel better when he hugged her. Dr. Pam, too. Maybe Saint Peter was right.

Hugs didn't cost anything at all, but they were sure nice to have.

"Don't look so glum," Lucky said. "It's almost time for Sweet Sigh to run in the third race."

"Will you be broke if Sweet Sigh doesn't win?"

"Not me. I make it a point not to bet any more than I can afford to lose."

"Guess I should have thought of that when I still had my two dollars."

"You probably will next time."

She leaned her head against Lucky's shoulder. She'd picked a real smart daddy. She sure hoped he'd let her be his little girl.

PAM HURRIED BACK from the rest room toward Lucky's box seats. As she approached, she noticed him talking to a man dressed in a rumpled blue suit that looked as if it hadn't been pressed in a year. They finished their conversation with a handshake just as she arrived, and the stranger wandered off.

"I haven't missed Sweet Sigh's start, have I?" she asked a little breathlessly.

He tossed her a quick smile. "They're about to announce the horses now."

"Are you nervous?"

"Yeah," he admitted. "My stomach fills with knots any time one of my horses is running. That's why I stay away from the horse barns before the race. I give my trainer and the jockeys a migraine if I hang around."

Laughing, she tucked her arm through his. He had Angie perched in front of him on the railing, and it looked as if he didn't plan to sit down at all until the race was over. Pam could understand that. She was feeling a little anxious herself, and it wasn't entirely because she had ten dollars riding on the outcome of the race.

When the horses paraded in front of the stands, Lucky's dark filly pranced around like she was the Queen of Sheba. His jockey's silks were the shade of Lucky's jacket, and on the back of his flowing shirt was a bright green four-leaf clover.

"No one would guess Sweet Sigh's owner believes in luck," she said wryly.

"Yeah, well, sometimes that's all you got going for you." He drew a nervous breath. "Now comes the hard part."

Once again, Pam found herself fascinated by the process of the horses entering the gates. Her heart moved up into her throat when Sweet Sigh shied, and the jockey had to walk her around to line her up with the gate again.

Pam's fingers closed tightly around Lucky's biceps. Beneath his jacket, his muscles felt like corded steel. She wanted him to hold her, to ease the thrumming tension that was building as her nerves grew taut. She'd rarely been so aware of a man—his leathery scent, his size and strength, and what she wanted to do with him.

"There they go!" Angie cried.

Pam clung more tightly to Lucky's arm.

By the time the horses reached the first turn, Sweet Sigh was running close to the inside rail, but far back in the pack, the leaders pulling away with each new stride.

"Lucky, she's in trouble," Pam said.

"Don't worry. The fast pace is going to cook the leaders. She'll catch 'em on the back stretch."

How did he know? The horse was losing ground by the minute, lengths behind the front runners, and Pam's ten-dollar bet looked as if it would evaporate into thin air. How could Lucky stand the tension? And the potential for a much greater financial loss?

Then, with steady determination, Sweet Sigh moved up on the leaders. She passed one horse after another until she was in striking distance of taking the lead. The PA announcer's voice rose in excitement.

"Oh, my gosh..." Pam's heart raced as fast as the horses. They rounded the last turn and headed for home. The crowd roared a deafening sound. The leaders were neck and neck, nose and nose. Pam could hardly breathe. Her throat ached from screaming.

"Come on, Sweet Sigh! You can do it!"

In a blur, the two lead horses thundered past the finish line so close together, Pam had no idea which one had won.

She looked up at Lucky. His triumphant smile told her all she needed to know.

Standing on tiptoe, she kissed him. She'd only meant it as a congratulatory peck. But he deepened the kiss, and their breaths tangled with excitement—the thrill of the race, the heat of mutual awareness, and the promise of more to come.

"Hey, do I get a hug, too?" Angie complained.

Lucky broke the kiss, but his gaze continued to cling to Pam's as he said, "Sure, sport." His eyes were dark with the promise he had communicated through his kiss. Pam's heart stuttered as she silently acknowledged she'd welcome the time he'd make good on his unspoken vow.

Tumult broke out an instant later as other owners in the stands congratulated Lucky. Among the applause and accolades, Pam was swept along as he made his way to the winner's circle with Angie in his arms. He looked for all the world like a proud papa showing off his daughter, and when he drew Pam into the circle of his arm, Pam felt a deep sense of belonging that she hadn't experienced since her childhood.

It was becoming increasingly difficult to remember they weren't really a family and that Lucky was absolutely the wrong man for her. Instead, it felt very much as if she were falling in love.

Flashbulbs flared as Lucky congratulated his jockey and accepted a trophy for Sweet Sigh's winning effort.

Another owner, one of the losers, joshed with Lucky, "You must have smeared a little extra scent on your filly's rump, Lucky. Our boys were chasing her so hard, she got scared and ran away from the field."

He grinned smugly. "Whatever works, I always say."

General laughter greeted his remark.

A distinguished gentleman wearing a silk lemon yellow, Western-cut shirt spoke to Pam. "I hope you'll be joining us at the Track Employees Benefit Gala the week after next, ma'am. Lucky is doing a fine job organizing the event."

"He is? I hadn't heard—"

"She'll be there," Lucky assured his friend. "I just haven't gotten around to inviting her yet."

She eyed him speculatively. "No, you haven't." In fact, he hadn't mentioned anything about organizing what sounded like a charitable event. Based on what Lucky had told Roger Peltam, he wasn't a joiner. But maybe that didn't apply when it came to helping those who populated his world—the world of horse racing.

Lucky set Angie down, and she scampered over to Rafael, who lifted her into his arms.

"Trust me, sweetheart, you'll have a great time at the ball," Lucky promised Pam. "We can even try our hand at slow dancing."

"I didn't think you did anything slowly," she quipped.

He let his gaze rove leisurely over her, heating her cheeks and generally raising her temperature by several degrees. "Yeah, there are a couple of things I don't like to rush. Dancing is only one of them."

She knew what else he wanted to take slowly. Desperately, she tried to repress the desire to hurry him along.

"THE HOUSE FEELS EMPTY without Angie here." Pam let Lucky help her out of her sweater in the front entryway of his house. It was well after dark and there was a damp chill in the air.

"You saw how excited she was to stay overnight at the racetrack. Kim, the groom she's bunking with, is a very reliable young lady. She'll watch out for Angie, and Rafael will bring her home in the morning."

That might be all very well and good, but who was going to look out for Pam until tomorrow? Ever since their celebratory kiss at the track, Pam's whole body had been resonating in anticipation of what would happen next. She hadn't been able to draw a steady breath all afternoon. And her pulse rate hadn't dropped below 150. Lord knew how elevated her blood pressure might be.

If something didn't happen soon, she was likely to have a cardiac incident. A serious one.

His fingertips lingered along the back of her neck. "Are you hungry?"

Very. For the flavor of his mouth, the salty taste of his skin. "I don't think so. Unless you are."

"I'm not hungry for anything I'd be likely to find in the kitchen."

Her nerves skittered around as if she'd been overdosed on caffeine. "Well, then . . ."

Taking her shoulders, he turned her so she was facing him. "We could watch television."

"Yes, I suppose we could. But I don't think there's anything particularly good on tonight." The breadth of his chest was far more interesting. Or the fascinating hint of a cleft in his chin.

"You want to talk about politics? Religion? The most intriguing adenoids you've ever seen?"

She swallowed hard. "I don't think so."

"Okay. How 'bout we make love until we come up with a better idea?"

Her head snapped up and she met his wickedly teasing, blue-eyed gaze. She wasn't being sensible. Nor was he. They both knew that. And it didn't matter. "That sounds like a reasonable idea. For starters," she said.

"Your bedroom or mine?"

She could feel a shudder start at her toes and work its way upward. "Yours, I think."

"You wanna race me up the stairs?"

She shook her head. Her wobbly legs probably wouldn't carry her across the room, much less upstairs.

"Good." In a fluid movement that spoke of both agility and strength, he slid one arm under her knees, the other behind her back, and picked her up. "I've always wanted to do this to a woman."

Gasping in surprise, and stifling a startled laugh, she linked her fingers behind his neck, threading them through the silken strands of his dark, unkempt hair. "You don't do this often?"

"Only in my dreams."

That was mildly reassuring. Though she was sure Lucky was capable of luring any woman he wanted into his lair.

Without even breaking a sweat, he carried her up the stairs and into his room.

His bedroom was filled with lush greens and dark mahogany, thick carpeting and a scent that Pam had grown to identify as specifically belonging to Lucky O'Toole. The combination nudged her libido into high gear. She wanted this man. She was obsessed with him.

"Like I promised, I want to take this real slow," he said, his fingers nudging her breasts as he unbuttoned her dress. "But I don't think I can."

She slid his jacket off and tugged his shirt from his pants. "I think I can keep up with you."

"Good." He dragged out the word, then lowered his head to lave her breasts through the lacy fabric of her bra. She nearly shattered into a thousand pieces at the first touch of his tongue. A moan ripped from her throat.

Without any semblance of finesse, he stripped her clothes away. She returned the favor with the same elemental urgency until she was finally able to see him, touch him—as she had dreamed about seeing and touching him since the first moment they'd met.

"You're magnificent," she whispered. Her fingers mapped the contours of his chest, then slid lower.

He groaned. "Ah, baby... I knew you'd be hot. So hot."

They tumbled onto the bed together, the velour spread bunching in their frenzied effort to explore and devour each other. His hands were rough and hard on her, as if he couldn't get enough, his tongue gentle and caressing. She writhed beneath him.

In spite of her own eager response, he made love to her with excruciating thoroughness. He found every one of her erogenous zones, excited sensitive nerve endings in ways that she hadn't thought possible. Never had her body been so alive, her heart so involved in an act that now defied description. This wasn't simply making love. This was climbing the steps to heaven. Breathlessly. Eagerly. With a partner who knew instinctively her every need.

He caressed her thighs, the backs of her knees, that secret nub that ached for his touch. Her nipples beaded when he suckled, grew chilled when his attentions drifted purposefully to alternate pleasure points.

Her fingers dug into his shoulders. She sobbed his name. Pleading. Demanding.

She arched her back as he finally plunged into her. She was beyond thought. Beyond knowing. Aware only of an insatiable need that he alone could fill, a pleasure he alone could provide.

Then need and pleasure erupted in cataclysmic wonder as they reached the highest step of their passion together and flew over the top, then settled slowly back to some modicum of reason.

Her body slick with perspiration, Lucky's weight a welcome burden, Pam sighed.

"That's it, Doc." Lucky groaned. "The sweetest sound in the world—the sigh of a well-satisfied woman."

If she'd had an ounce of energy left, she would have smiled.

Drained of every bit of his strength, Lucky lay with his head on Pam's breast. Her flesh was damp, her body shuddering every few moments. Slowly his heartbeat eased to match the pace he felt beneath his ear.

He figured that had been about the wildest ride he'd ever experienced. Normally, he was able to stay under control. Slow and easy, so the woman had plenty of time to enjoy the experience. Not this time.

He hadn't been particularly gentle. But with every thrust, she'd met him more than halfway. They were dynamite together. Just as he'd known they would be.

So that should have taken care of the craving that had been gnawing at him since he first saw her at the hospital. At least his wanting her should have held off for a half hour or so.

But it hadn't.

"I think we've got a problem, Doc."

"Hmm?"

"Looks like I may be interested in a repeat performance. Soon."

She shifted beneath him, and need rocketed through him one more time. "I thought you'd never ask. What took you so long?"

Laughing, he reversed their positions. "Okay, smart aleck. This time you do all the hard work and we'll see how long it takes you to recover."

"The pleasure would be all mine, Mr. O'Toole."

USING HER KEY, Pam opened the back door to the clinic the next morning and hurried inside. She grabbed her lab jacket from the coatrack.

Irma Sue met her in the hallway. "You're late."

"Sorry. Have we got a big crowd waiting?"

"Enough to hold a Beatles concert and make a profit."

"I'll work fast. I promise."

Eyeing her with interest, Irma Sue handed Pam the first patient's chart. "You look happy."

"Of course. I love being a doctor."

"Uh-uh." Irma Sue's dark eyes gleamed. She was too perceptive by far. "How's the pizza man?"

Delicious. Every little bite. "He's fine. His horse won yesterday."

"That a fact?"

"Irma Sue, are you planning to swallow that canary soon so I can get on with my work?"

The nurse held up her hands in mock surrender. "Yes, ma'am, Dr. Pam. I was just trying to remember the last time I saw you glowin' like that. It sure must have been some fine horse race."

Her glow quickly changing to a full-fledged blush, Pam gave up all pretense of saving face. "It was the best, Irma Sue. *Now* can we get to work?"

"Ooo-eee, I knew that pizza man was gonna be just what the doctor ordered."

Pam rolled her eyes. Keeping a secret from Irma Sue was like trying to slow down a rising tide. But she was right. The night with Lucky had been a revelation.

Never had Pam experienced such dizzying heights of passion. She hadn't thought it possible. Everything that had gone before paled in comparison to the sensual delights Lucky had taught her.

It was as though Ted, with all of his degrees and credentials, had been a rank amateur when it came to pleasing a woman. How strange she hadn't realized that until now. Perhaps the respect she'd had for her husband had masked the possibility that he wasn't perfect.

The day passed in a whirl of patients and medical charts, prescriptions and well-baby checkups. All the while, a nonsensical tune hummed on her lips, a lightheartedness filled her chest, and Irma Sue kept on slanting knowing looks in Pam's direction.

Even at the end of the day, when she caught a glimpse of herself in a mirror, Pam could still see a glow on her cheeks. She was ready to see Lucky again, ready to head for home.

Home. Her throat constricted around the word.

Lucky's house wasn't her home. She owned a conservative town house in a conservative neighborhood with guarded gates and tons of security. The members of the church and most of the civic leaders respected her, as they had her husband. With the one exception of a ten dollar bet yesterday, she'd never gambled in her life. The thought of risking as much as a hundred dollars made her break out in a cold sweat.

Lucky took that kind of risk every day simply by raising and breeding horses.

Yet he was the lover every woman dreamed about—
the one she had never even allowed herself to think
about. Fantasies didn't come true. Only hard work
could give shape to a dream. Hadn't her family proven
that time and again through a long string of shining
failures and shattered illusions?

SHE TURNED INTO the drive at Lucky's place and was
forced to maneuver around an old Mercedes sedan
parked in front of the steps. Lucky was talking with the
man she had seen at the racetrack, who was still wearing the same rumpled suit.

Plucking her purse and a medical journal from the
passenger seat, she got out of her car. A few raindrops
splattered onto the drive. As she walked toward Lucky,
she saw him peel off several bills from his money clip
and hand them to the stranger.

An awful array of thoughts crossed her mind. Had he
lost that much money on a side bet? Or had Sweet Sigh
won because the race had been fixed, and Lucky was
now paying off the man who had carried out the nefar-
ious scheme? Or maybe a racehorse owner had to pay
for protection?

Her stomach churned at the possibilities. The business of horse racing was so far out of her experience—
and so filled with risks unknown to her—she didn't
know what to think.

The stranger tipped his hat toward her. "Evening,
ma'am."

She smiled, though it felt like a clown's plastic imitation stretching her lips.

Lucky shook the stranger's hand. "Take care of yourself, Howard."

"I will . . . and thanks."

"Don't worry about it. I owe ya."

With that, the stranger returned to his car, backed around, and drove away.

Pam sent Lucky a questioning look.

"An old friend," he said.

"To whom you owed a great deal of money?"

"I owe him my friendship. For me, that's more important."

"It looked like a pretty expensive payoff to me."

His brows lowered into a frown. "Howard Rosenberg used to own a string of horses. Damn good ones, too. Once, when I was a kid, he gave me a break. Recently he's had some bad luck and has pretty nearly lost everything. I don't know about you, lady, but I don't forget my friends when they need me."

Pam felt as if she'd been punched in the stomach, and she hugged her midsection. She probably deserved his scolding tone but she couldn't help herself. Their relationship was so new and terribly unsettling. "I'm sorry."

"What did you think was going on?"

"I thought . . ." She'd misjudged Lucky. He hadn't been fixing races or placing illegal side bets. He'd been helping a friend who was down on his luck, a racehorse owner who had gone broke. A man who had no doubt been very much like Lucky once, riding high on the hog with a pocket full of money, fancy cars and a mansion to call his own. All of which he'd lost.

Swallowing hard, she raised her gaze to meet his. "I can't do this, Lucky. I'm sorry."

"Do what?"

"I know I agreed to stay here with you and Angie until—" The words stuck like razor blades in her throat. "And I will stay, but I can't . . . I mean—"

He moved in on her. Close. So close she caught his leather-and-spice scent. "Are you talkin' about limiting us to a one-night stand?"

"That's not exactly—"

"Then what, sweetheart?" Lifting her chin, he rasped his thumb along her lower lip.

She couldn't think when he touched her that way, when he was standing so close, when her whole being wanted him with such frenzied need. Her desire for him battered against her good reason, pummeling at the very foundations of her existence. They were so totally unsuited for each other, yet she had never felt so alive as when she'd been in his arms.

How could she possibly explain? To him? To herself? She didn't dare try to grab a dream that was no more than smoke. If only he could see the background she'd come from, surely he'd understand how much she needed security. It would be clear that building a life on the dream of a two-dollar bet simply couldn't work for her.

"Would you be willing to meet my parents?" she asked, her voice quaking with conflicting emotions.

One side of his mouth hitched into a half smile. "Name the day."

Chapter Nine

Lucky stepped out of Pam's car and looked up the hill toward the house where her parents lived. His eyes widened. A woman wearing a flowing white cape was dangling from an aerial wire and sliding toward him at about a hundred miles per hour. Smiling broadly, she looked like a circus performer who was having a hell of a good time.

"I gather that's your mother," he said when Pam joined him beside the car.

"I'm afraid so. When I phoned to let them know we were coming, she said she'd gotten a stunt job for some action movie. She's probably practicing."

"Terrific. Looks like fun."

"It's dangerous," Pam said with undisguised concern. "She could break her neck." At least if that happened now there'd be a doctor nearby. Which was why Pam had invested a good many years in medical training.

Monica Jones dropped to her feet right in front of Pam and opened her arms wide. A little breathlessly, she said, "Pammy, honey, I'm so glad to see you."

Lucky grinned. *Pammy?* He'd have to remember that.

"Hi, Mom." Pam returned the embrace. "Don't you think you're just a little too—"

"Don't you dare say I'm too old! The casting office thinks I'm perfect for the job, and nobody's gonna tell 'em different. If I'm able to handle this stunt, then no telling what other jobs they'll call me for." Monica turned toward Lucky. "And this must be your young man."

"Mom, no, he's not—"

"Lucky O'Toole." He extended his hand. "Now that I've met you, Mrs. Jones, I can certainly see where Pam gets her beauty."

Monica flushed with pleasure. "Aren't you sweet."

Under her breath, Pam said, "And we all know about your glib Irish tongue."

"One of those things you love best about me," he replied just as privately. Though he hadn't had much chance to use his tongue in any interesting ways for the past couple of days, since they'd made love that one night—all night. Pam had gone back to being distant and downright testy at times. It had irritated him like crazy but he hadn't been able to entice her back into his bed. Not that he'd given up trying...

Linking her arm through Lucky's, Monica said, "Come on up to the house, young man. And please call me Monica. *Mrs.* makes me feel so ancient."

"You don't look in the least old to me, Monica. Why, if I weren't already involved with your daughter—"

"We're *not* involved," Pam whispered behind his back.

"Young man, you do wonders for a woman's ego." She laughed, a full-bodied sound, as though enjoying life was what she did best. "I can certainly understand why Pammy wanted us to meet you."

They walked up the stairs together in a fairly conventional manner. Eyeing the aerial wire and a trampoline off in a side yard, plus Monica's odd costume, Lucky suspected walking was one of the few things the Jones family did that would seem ordinary. He rather liked that. And could understand why it drove Pam absolutely bonkers.

Standing at the bottom of the steep stairs that led up to the house, Pam drew a discouraged breath. She should have known her mother and Lucky would get along famously. They were two of a kind. She'd brought Lucky here to demonstrate how eccentric her family was and, therefore, how important it was to her to live a normal, well-respected life. Ted had understood that.

Obviously, Lucky didn't.

As she started up the steps, she noticed that a big, blue tarp covered half the roof of the house. "Mom, I thought you said Dad was going to get the roof fixed."

"Oh, he will, dear. He's been so busy, he simply hasn't had time."

Right. It was December. The rainy season was nearly upon them. In fact, storms had been crowding Southern California for days without producing any measurable precipitation. But they would. Soon. And her father hadn't gotten around to fixing the leaky roof.

Typical.

It was just as well they'd left Angie with Rafael. Whenever Pam was around her parents, she developed a severe migraine. She wouldn't have wanted to deal with a six-year-old, who'd no doubt be happy to go sailing down the high wire with her pseudofoster grandmother. Besides, explaining the child would have been far too difficult.

Making her parents understand her relationship with Lucky was going to be hard enough. Particularly since she didn't understand it herself.

Good grief, how she'd wanted to go to his bed every night since they'd made love. She had forced herself to resist the urge, at the penalty of a good many sleepless hours. Not that she'd ever admit it to him. Or to her parents.

Her father stepped out onto the porch and waved. A tall man with prominent features and a straight back, he might have once played romantic leads, if he'd had enough talent, but now his eyebrows had gone bushy, his face more craggy than handsome.

"Forsooth!" he called in a sonorous baritone. "'Tis the joy of my life, the fruit of my loins, beloved daughter Pamela, returned at last."

"Hi, Daddy."

"You know me well," he quoted, bowing slightly. "I am he."

She smiled weakly, suspecting a Shakespearean character had been added to his repertoire. She reached the porch and he gave her a rib-crushing hug. The sweet scent of pipe tobacco clung to his wool shirt, reminding her of a thousand cherished nights during her childhood when she'd crawled up into his lap to listen to him read a story.

Releasing her, Jimmy Jones eyed Lucky speculatively. "And what yon rogue is this, I pray thee?"

"Daddy, please—" She stopped herself. There was no way she could get her father to act normally. She doubted he even knew after the many roles he'd played—or wanted to play—what "normal" was. So she introduced Lucky and hoped for the best as they all went inside.

Though it might not be apparent to anyone else, Pam could tell her mother had made an effort to straighten up the living room, and she blessed her for it. Months' worth of *Variety* had been neatly stacked beside the frayed couch instead of scattered all around the room, and the usual clutter of discarded sweaters and socks had been removed.

"Did your mother tell you the good news?" her father asked.

"What's that?"

"They're going to be redoing *Macbeth* for the big screen and I'm reading for a part." Making a fist, he crossed his arm over his chest. "Methought I heard a cry, 'Sleep no more!'" he entoned dramatically. "'Macbeth does murder sleep, the innocent sleep—'"

"That's great, Dad."

Monica smiled her approval. "He makes a wonderful Macbeth, doesn't he, dear? I think it's entirely possible that he should have been playing Shakespeare all along. He has such a flair."

"It's the break I've been waiting for," Jimmy agreed. "I'm sure of it."

Pam wasn't nearly as confident. Too many breaks had evaporated into smoke over the years for her to get her hopes up now. And she wished her parents wouldn't, either.

Settling into his big, overstuffed chair, Jimmy said, "Now then, Lucky, tell us about yourself. Do you go to the movies often?"

Only in her family would a possible suitor be questioned about his movie-going preferences, Pam mused as she sat down on the couch and signaled Lucky to join her.

"I used go to a lot when I was younger," Lucky said. "But I've kind of gotten out of the habit lately."

"It's still great entertainment, you know. Maybe you've seen something Monica or I played in. Between us, we've got fifty-seven screen credits. Impressive, uh?"

"It is," Lucky agreed. "In fact, I gotta say your voice has a familiar ring to it. Like I know you from somewhere."

Jimmy reeled off a dozen movie titles before Lucky snapped his thumb and forefinger together and said, "That's it! *Alien Apeman*. I must have seen that movie six or seven times when I was a kid. It was great."

Wincing, Pam knew she was going to have to throw in the towel. Clearly, Lucky loved her parents and their unconventional life-style. She could see it in his eyes as he reminisced with her father about *Alien Apeman*, then joshed her mother into describing some of her most death-defying stunts. The three of them were getting along famously.

Clearing the press of despair from her throat, she interrupted, asking after her brother. "Mom, I thought maybe Reggie would be here. I haven't talked to him in weeks."

"Oh no, dear. Didn't I tell you? He left last weekend. He and his band had a chance to go on tour."

"The kid's a real trouper," her father said, beaming. "Just like his old man. He and his buddies crammed into an old Fiat, strapped their instruments on top and headed for Fort Lauderdale. That's where their gig is."

"In Florida?" Pam nearly choked on the question. "Dad, he's supposed to be in school. He's going to miss his finals. I agreed to pay for his books and fees at the community college so he—"

"This could be his big break, Pammy. He had to go."

"Fort Lauderdale is a great town," Lucky added. "It sounds like your brother isn't ready to start letting any moss grow on his feet."

Pam's heart sank. Once again she was the odd man out. Why couldn't she fit in with her own family as easily as Lucky did?

Whatever the reason, it was a clear indication she and Lucky had no hope of a future together. And she might as well get used to that idea right now. After all, she'd known it from the beginning.

Tears clogged her throat and she didn't know why the truth should hurt so much.

"I'll fix us some coffee," she said, standing and excusing herself before she turned into a blubbering fool.

"You don't have to do that, dear," her mother said distractedly. "I'll take care of it."

But her mother didn't. Instead, Pam washed out the pot, filled it with fresh water, and found the grounds in the cupboard. Her mother had never learned that coffee simply didn't make itself. Or maybe she had never cared.

LUCKY WAS BEGINNING to figure Pam had been in the kitchen so long that she'd actually gone to Brazil for the coffee beans. As much as he was enjoying himself with her parents, he went in search of her.

She was standing on the back porch, her fingers wrapped around a coffee mug, gazing at an overgrown hillside littered with an assortment of trash—old tires, a tattered cardboard box filled with recyclable plastic bottles, a rope swing that had seen better days, and the remnants of a playhouse.

"Reliving your childhood?" he asked softly.

She turned, and the sad look of vulnerability in her eyes slammed into Lucky's gut. He wanted nothing more than to hold her in his arms and bring cheer to a determined spirit that was far too close to burnout. But he sensed she wouldn't welcome his sympathy. Stubborn woman!

"In a way, I guess."

"Your folks are pretty terrific. I envy you."

"Envy? I can't tell you how ashamed I used to be of Dad playing in those awful B movies. I still feel guilty for feeling that way."

"Don't. Kids are never as impressed with their folks as other people are."

"But if they had only—"

"'If onlys' don't work either, Pam. They're living their life the way they want to. You can't change that."

She stared down into her cup. "I guess other little girls dreamed of having a fairy godmother. I used to dream of having a father who was an incredibly dull, boring banker. Or maybe a shoe salesman. Not someone who thought one week he was going to be the next Marlon Brando, and right after that he'd start in on a Anthony Quinn routine. Now he's a Shakespearean actor."

Lucky laughed. "The secret is to be happy with whatever cards you're dealt. That's a tough lesson to learn. Besides, look at it this way." He lifted her chin. "Your folks are honest, aren't they?"

"Of course."

"They've never robbed a bank or done drugs?"

"Certainly not." Instinctively she leaped to their defense. "They're just a little...different."

"But they loved you and your brother and sister?"

The guilt of being far too judgmental when it came to her parents prickled through her conscience. "Always. None of us ever doubted that."

"Then maybe, now that you're all grown up, you ought to cut them a little slack. Some kids are a lot less fortunate than you were."

She knew Lucky was right. Through his eyes, her parents were rightfully head and shoulders above his, since, as he must have seen it, they had deserted him. She wondered how he had survived the feeling of abandonment. "Even though your childhood was terrible in many ways, you managed so well. How did you do it?"

"Mostly, I did it one day at a time. The fact is, I've got a handful of aces right now," he admitted. "All of that could change, and I think I'd still figure life was pretty darn good."

Catching her lower lip between her teeth, she said, "I can't live like that, Lucky. Old habits, old fears die hard for me. I need to *know* there's plenty of money to put food on the table. I need to be able to walk down the street and know I have the respect of those I meet."

"And you figure hanging around with a racetrack honcho doesn't qualify for much respect."

"I didn't mean that . . . exactly."

"I think you did." He brushed a quick kiss against her lips. "And I think you're missing a whole hell of a lot of fun, too. Fun that you desperately want to be a part of. You figure the only thing worthwhile is the initials after a guy's name. You want roses and poetry, like your husband gave you, and I'm a down and dirty kind of guy. But I'm tellin' you, Doc, there's something between us that can't be measured by smooth talk or a pinstriped suit. Or even a stethoscope. Whether you admit it or not, we're ridin' the same roller coaster. And I'm going to prove it to you."

If anyone could, Lucky would be the man. In her heart of hearts, a place she didn't dare acknowledge, Pam hoped he was right.

HE SHOWED UP at the clinic the next day a little after twelve with a huge bouquet of Christmas holly—the prickly, thorny kind with big red berries. A teasing, devil-may-care smile creased his cheeks.

Pam tried unsuccessfully to quash the secret thrill of finding him in the clinic's waiting room, in spite of the fact that she'd seen him across the breakfast table that morning, and he'd dogged her footsteps the previous evening after their return from her parents' house. An impossible man to get rid of, he simply wouldn't take no for an answer. And she hated that a part of her was glad.

"I guess the waiting room could use a little sprucing up for Christmas," she said, accepting the decorative offering with as much cool aplomb as she could manage. Except for the two of them, the clinic was empty, uncharacteristically quiet between the morning and afternoon rush of patients. Even Irma Sue was gone, taking advantage of the break to do a little Christmas shopping of her own.

"Actually, what I have in mind is to make you think of me anytime you see a sprig of holly."

"And roses aren't your style," she said wryly.

"Nope. I try to be more original than that."

He had that right. Lucky O'Toole was definitely one of a kind—as unpredictable and rough edged as the bouquet he'd chosen.

Crowding inside her personal space, he said, "So are you going to thank me with a kiss?"

Her heart struck an errant beat and she backed away. "No, I'm going to find something so I can put the holly in water. I wouldn't want it to wilt," she said pointedly.

Sputtering a laugh, he followed her toward the back of the building. "Those two activities—kissing and finding a vase—aren't mutually exclusive."

"I have difficulty concentrating on more than one task at a time," she replied over her shoulder.

"Then we'll compromise. We'll skip the holly and get right to the kissing part."

"Sorry, that's not an option I care to consider." She'd told him they had no future together. He hadn't gotten the message. Regretfully, in her heart, neither had she.

In the storeroom, she placed the holly on the counter and opened a cupboard to search for something resembling a vase. Her skin tingled with an electric awareness of Lucky's proximity. She'd been struggling against her attraction to him for days, all the more so since they had made love, and she'd vowed not to repeat her foolish behavior. With each successive minute, she seemed to be losing the battle—both with him and with herself.

He closed the storeroom door to the hallway and jammed a chair under the doorknob.

Her eyes widened. "What are you doing?"

His gaze swept over her. Slowly. Suggestively. "Did your husband ever make love to you here in the storeroom?"

Her pulse jumped. "Of course not. This is a medical facility."

"The idea has a certain amount of appeal though, doesn't it?"

"It does not," she lied. The wicked glint in his laughing Irish eyes had appeal. The sensual shape of his lips had appeal. His natural charm and charisma, and everything else about Lucky O'Toole had an irresistible appeal, including the impossible idea of making love to him in a storeroom filled with such oddities as paper gowns, latex gloves and patient charts. But she wasn't going to tell him that.

Giving the narrow room a quick appraisal, he said, "I figure we'll have to do it standing up."

"We what?" She pictured herself with her back pressed against a row of shelves, her legs wrapped around his waist, her fingers wantonly tangling in his hair—an image that nearly stole her breath away. "I've never..."

"It always adds a little zest to make love in unconventional places. *If* you're an unconventional kind of person, that is."

"I'm very conventional."

"That makes it even better."

While she'd been imagining what he was thinking about, Lucky had edged closer again. His spicy scent mingled with medicinal smells of the clinic that she had never thought of as arousing—until now. Combined, they drugged her common sense.

"Of course," he continued, "part of the thrill is thinking someone might try to get in the storeroom while we're doing it." His fingertips caressed her cheek; his thumb rasped the outline of her lower lip.

She swallowed thickly. "Irma Sue will be gone for another forty-five minutes." Now why had she told him that when she ought to be running for her life?

With infinite slowness, his fingers slid to the back of her head, massaging lightly. "The waiting room might fill up with patients while we're doing it."

She trembled at the thought. "The front door is locked."

"Then there isn't any reason why we shouldn't enjoy ourselves."

Pam was sure there were lots of reasons. She simply couldn't think of one at the moment, not while his lips were covering hers, his tongue testing her resistance and finding only complete surrender.

At his house, she was on guard, careful to avoid even his casual touch or the possibility of intimacy. She hadn't been prepared for his incredible audacity. No one had ever wanted to make love to her here, in her office, on her turf, his fingers skillfully removing her blouse, hiking up her skirt, finding intimate pathways to private places. Erotic places. Sliding past layers of nylon, he discovered a tiny nub of sensitive nerves with his fingertip. His calluses created exquisite sensations that rippled through her body, making her gasp at the sheer hedonistic pleasure of having him touch her in that way.

Her defenses in disarray, she clung to him. The swift pulsing of her blood roared in her ears.

"This is crazy," she whispered when he dragged his open, hungry mouth from hers.

"Yeah. I know." He stripped her stockings away. Her underpants followed. "Great, isn't it?" The snap on his jeans snicked open; the zipper purred downward. In glorious, full arousal, his manhood appeared.

"Yes." The word escaped her in a sob as he entered her with a swift, sure thrust.

This was more than crazy. It was insane and foolish, the most imprudent thing Pam had ever done. And the most exciting. In her frenzied desire to get closer to Lucky, to take in all of him, she lifted her legs and wrapped them around his waist. His jeans abraded the tender flesh of her inner thighs. She gasped and pulled him tighter.

"Hurry," she urged him.

"There's no rush, Doc." He groaned and drove himself into her again. "We've got all the time in the world."

"Lunch hour—"

"Eternity."

He was huge inside her, stretching her in unendurable, impossibly erotic ways. Her body convulsed around his. She tried to stifle her cry of pleasure by burying her head at the juncture of his neck and shoulder. In return, she tasted the salty flavor of his skin and felt the gush of his release exploding deeply within her. Her body pulsed again and his hoarse cry enveloped her soul as completely as his arms enclosed her.

She lay limply, weightlessly in Lucky's arms. If he'd had to describe what had just happened between them, he would have failed dismally. He didn't have the words. He doubted the greatest poet in the world could have expressed the awe and reverence he felt. As nearly as he could tell, he'd had a glimpse of heaven.

He sprinkled kisses over Pam's flushed cheeks as her legs slid down his body and she stood a little unsteadily. Her eyes fluttered open. Her pupils were dilated and she had a soft, dreamy look about her. A kissable look.

"So what do you think?" His lips hitched into a smile.

"I think you're certifiable, O'Toole. We both are. In a storeroom?"

"We could try an examining room next. There's still plenty of time—"

"Nobody's that quick."

"I'll give you eight-to-five—"

She yanked on his ear, but not very hard.

Slipping away from him, she retrieved her bikini briefs. Beneath her professional image lay a woman who liked soft, feminine garb—lacy and sexy. Lucky liked that. He liked a whole lot about Pamela Jones.

"You ripped my panty hose," she complained, frowning.

"I'll buy you a new pair." He zipped and snapped his jeans.

"I've got a spare set in my office. The problem is, how do I get to them? I just heard the back door close. That means Irma Sue has returned from her shopping expedition."

"You want me to go get 'em?"

She laughed a choked sound. "Not a chance. I'm going to have enough trouble on my own explaining what we've been doing in here for the last half hour."

In a reverse striptease, combined with a one-legged balancing act, she tugged her stockings up over slim, trim ankles and legs. Just about everything Pam did sent Lucky's libido into high gear. He doubted he'd ever get enough of this woman.

She had just finger-combed her hair into a tousled semblance of order when the door to the storeroom rattled.

"Move the chair," Pam whispered. She straightened her skirt and checked her blouse.

Grinning, Lucky quickly complied.

Irma Sue pushed through the door. Her eyes rounded.

"Oh, hi, Irma Sue. Back from your shopping already?" Pam asked, peering innocently up into the cupboard. "We were just looking for something to put this holly in. Lucky brought it to liven up the waiting room. Beautiful for the holidays, don't you think?"

Lucky winked at Pam. "And after you find a vase," he said confidentially, "we're gonna go take a look at the nearest examining room."

Pam whirled. Bright color rode her finely sculpted cheeks "We're not doing any such thing!"

"Ooo-eee!" Laughing, Irma Sue slapped her hand to her thigh. "I do believe the two of you had one heck of an interesting lunch hour."

"The best!" Lucky agreed.

Chapter Ten

Mortified.

That's how Pam felt the rest of the afternoon. She caught Irma Sue's telling looks; worried that her patients would somehow suspect what she'd been up to during her all-too-brief lunch hour.

Every time she stepped into an examining room, she pictured herself making love with Lucky on the paper-covered table. Cramped. Precarious. Incredibly exciting. She declared the storeroom entirely off-limits because she knew exactly what she'd think about if she walked across that particular threshold.

A niggling sense of guilt nudged at her conscience. Had she betrayed her husband by making love in the clinic that had been his dream? That they'd both worked so hard to create? Since Lucky had appeared in her life, the aching sense of loss had eased considerably. Was she being disloyal to Ted? Or was this a normal part of grief recovery?

Or even more disturbing, had the emotion she'd felt for Ted been no more than a deep sense of respect for his medical skills, not love?

By the time she finished her last appointment and hurried across the street to the hospital to check on a newborn, her thoughts were swirling in confusion. Breathlessly, she reached the nurses' station.

She stared aghast at the huge spray of Christmas holly on the counter.

"Hi, Dr. Pam. Isn't that a beautiful arrangement," the floor nurse said, admiring the bright green leaves and red berries accented with white ribbon. "Lucky brought it in for us. He certainly is a dynamite guy."

"Yes, he is," she agreed through clenched teeth. The man wasn't going to let her forget her moment of weakness. Not for a minute. She'd already spotted— and ignored—a similar spray of holly at the reception desk downstairs. He was everywhere, his trail of holly sprays a constant reminder to how eagerly she had broken her vow of keeping the man at arm's length.

The trail led right to his front door where garlands of holly branches decorated the porch. She groaned as new images popped into her mind. Him. Her. Doing it on the front porch! A titillating possibility, she admitted, then tried to quash the thought.

All smiles, Lucky and Angie met her in the entry hall.

"I gather you've cornered the market on holly," she said dryly, shedding her jacket.

"I figure it's a good investment. I expect to get an excellent return."

She shot him a quelling look in the hope of erasing his self-satisfied smile. It didn't work. And her heart pumped an extra beat because he was so darn sure of himself.

Angie took her hand and tugged her toward the living room. "Come see what Lucky got us, Dr. Pam. It's *gihugeic!* The biggest one in the whole, wide world."

"What is it, honey?"

"A tree!" Releasing Pam's hand, Angie ran across the room to stand in front of a Christmas tree that was nearly as tall as the cathedral ceiling.

Stunned, Pam told Lucky, "You don't know how to do things halfway, do you?"

"Nope. Not when it comes to important stuff."

He casually slipped his arm around her waist, and she got the distinct impression seducing her was included in his idea of "important stuff."

"Angie helped me string the lights," he said, "but we wanted to wait for you before we did the ornaments. I've got a pizza in the oven so we can decorate the tree and stuff ourselves at the same time."

"Sounds like you have everything planned."

He slanted her speculative glance. "Down to the last detail."

A current of heat started somewhere low in Pam's midsection and radiated outward. Lord, with only a wicked look and a few well-chosen words, he had the power to turn her on. Or maybe she was still simmering from their impulsive lunchtime tryst. "Give me a chance to change clothes," she pleaded as she made her escape. "I won't be long."

When she returned a few minutes later, dressed in slacks and tennis shoes, Angie was examining the boxes of ornaments stacked near the tree. Since Lucky wasn't in sight, Pam presumed he was in the kitchen preparing their pizza extravaganza.

Angie sighed wistfully. "They're sure pretty, aren't they?"

"Yes, they are." Pam sat down on the carpet next to her.

"I'm gonna be real careful not to break any of Lucky's orn'ments."

"I think he bought them because of you." The boxes, purchased from the most expensive department store at the mall, still had the price tags on them.

"But I already got into trouble once today. I don't want to make him mad again."

Pam raised her eyebrows. "What happened?"

"I washed his car."

"That seems like a nice thing for you to do."

"It was s'posed to be. But I forgot to wash off the soap. It left spots."

Pam winced. "On his Ferrari?" His pride and joy?

"I didn't mean to mess up again."

"I'm sure he knows that, honey. What did he say?"

She lifted her narrow shoulders in a shrug. "He made me wash his car all over again. 'Cept this time, he showed me how and helped me polish it real, real good."

Pulling Angie into her lap, Pam wrapped her arms around the child. She'd already put on a few pounds since she'd been living with Lucky and felt less like an undernourished waif. Her hair smelled sweet and her cheeks had a healthy glow. "Well, it doesn't sound to me like Lucky stayed mad at you for very long."

Angie considered Pam's conclusion for a moment. "I still think I better be careful. I don't want Lucky to send me away."

Pam doubted there was much chance of that but she was reluctant to make any promises. It was still possible the police chief would locate Angie's family. That would be a terrible blow to Lucky's plans and Angie's dreams. And would have a shattering impact on the unfocused image of the three of them together, a family portrait Pam was afraid to solidify in her own imagination.

"Okay, gang, one pizza with everything except anchovies," Lucky announced as he returned to the living room. "A little vino for two and one large milk. How's that?" He placed a large tray on the coffee table.

Pam nearly choked. Planted right smack in the middle of the pizza was a single sprig of bright green holly, including berries. Her gaze snapped up to meet Lucky's. The devil! Now he'd have her thinking about making love the whole time they were decorating the tree, as if the topic hadn't already been too much on her mind.

"You're a sneak, O'Toole," she accused him. "A low-down, underhanded—"

"Yeah. Don't you love it?"

She laughed. There seemed to be little else she could do in the face of his audacity. In fact, she laughed so much as the evening progressed and ornaments filled the tree, she wondered when she'd last had such a good time. Or if she ever had.

They saved the angel for the top of the tree until the very last. Lucky climbed up the ladder, steadying Angie in front of him.

"Don't let me fall, Lucky. I don't want to break the tree."

"Don't worry, sport. I've got you."

Very carefully, Angie placed the angel right where it belonged.

Tears thickened in Pam's throat and her chin quivered. This was what being a family was all about.

Soon after an elaborate lighting ceremony filled with ooo's and ahh's, Pam took Angie up to bed and tucked her in. When she returned, Lucky was sitting in a darkened room admiring the twinkling tree lights.

He extended his hand and she took it, settling down beside him on the floor with the couch for a backrest.

"Pretty terrific, huh?" He gazed at the tree like a little boy who was waiting eagerly for Santa to arrive.

"Yes, you are."

"I meant the tree."

"I know."

He cocked his head. "Do I detect signs that my irrepressible personality is beginning to wear you down?"

"I'm just being honest. You're the best thing that has ever happened to Angie. She told me that some of the foster homes where she lived didn't even have a tree at Christmas, much less one that is so *gihugeic.*" She drank the last few drops of wine from the glass she'd left on the end table.

"Yeah, I lived in places like that. But most of 'em tried to do something nice to make the holidays okay, and the orphanage always made a big deal about Santa Claus, not that any of us older kids believed in him. It wasn't like having your own family anyway."

"How . . . did your parents die?"

"I don't know. The cops found me wandering around a shopping mall in Pittsburgh. I was about four years old and all I knew for sure was my name."

She frowned. "What is your name?" Until now, she'd only known him as Lucky, and it was hard to imagine him with any other name.

"Patrick Terence O'Toole, at your service, madam." He nodded at the official introduction.

"Quite a mouthful for a four-year-old."

"Most of the time they called me P.T."

"Have you ever tried to locate your family?"

He poured a little more wine into her glass and took some himself. "I used to think about trying to find them when I was a kid, but after a while I decided they probably had a good reason for dumping me at the mall. So I left it alone."

Pam suspected somewhere in his little boy's heart, he'd always been afraid being abandoned had been his fault. Children took such terrible burdens on their small shoulders. She'd seen that in divorce cases when the kids had taken the blame for their parents separating and had actually made themselves sick. The same thing often happened when a sibling had died.

Pam wished she could make Lucky's past okay, but knew that wasn't any more possible for him than it was for the children she treated.

Quietly, they sat together in the glow from the Christmas lights. In the background, carols played on the stereo. The air felt heavy with intimacy and anticipation. Pam's pulse beat thickly through her veins.

She took another sip of wine, then set the glass back on the end table. "It's late. I've got work tomorrow."

"Yeah. Me, too."

He didn't make a move on her. They were sitting so close, shoulder to shoulder, she could feel his heat. But with irritating determination, he continued to stare at the tree, the lights flashing a kaleidoscope of color across his strong Irish profile.

"You want me to wash up the dirty dishes?" she asked.

"No, I'll take care of 'em."

So much for romantic interludes, she thought grimly, repressing a sigh. "Well, good night."

He didn't say a word as she got up and left the room. Not one word. Any reasonable woman would have expected a good-night kiss at the very least, given how they'd spent the lunch hour. But not O'Toole. Clearly, he was set on making her crazy.

She switched the light on and marched into her bedroom. Her feet came to a sudden halt.

The bed was turned down and a sprig of holly rested in the middle of her pillow. Now when had he done that? she wondered. When she'd come up to change clothes—

"I know making love in a bed is a bit conventional, but I thought we could give it a try."

She whirled. He was standing in the doorway, an elbow leaning against the doorjamb, a smug grin on his face.

She swallowed hard and futilely tried to slow her accelerating heart rate. He really was an impossibly arrogant man. "What about Angie? I wouldn't want—"

"She's sound asleep. And in case you hadn't noticed, there's a lock on your door." Stepping inside, he demonstrated how well the lock worked with the door closed.

"Lucky, I—"

"I know. This is a great way to end a terrific day."

She couldn't deny he was right about that. But somewhere in the back of her mind she knew they'd spent the evening pretending to be a family. Now she and Lucky were playing at the game of being lovers.

The world of make-believe had always belonged to her parents. Pam was the one who was supposed to keep her feet solidly on the ground. For the moment, however, she couldn't seem to find her footing.

THE PRETENSE CONTINUED for the next week, and reality grew less and less important. For the first time in Pam's life she could understand how her father could dream about making it big in the movies—or in life. Her fantasy was no less implausible.

She and Lucky were totally unsuited for each other. He never seemed to take anything seriously—except his horses and the Ferarri. She worried constantly over the financial state of the clinic—recently improved by Lucky's generous contributions, she admitted—and how to entice her brother into going back to school.

But when she was with Lucky, she developed a bad case of amnesia, her troubles forgotten as she feasted on a delicious combination of laughter and passion.

Pam knew it couldn't last.

The doorbell rang as she sat curled up at the end of the couch after a long day at the clinic. Her feet ached and her back was tired; she'd felt uncharacteristically weary for the past couple of days, lack of sleep obviously a contributing factor. Lucky was at an Association of Racehorse Owners meeting making last minute plans for the upcoming gala for the Track Employees Welfare Foundation, and she'd just gotten Angie to bed. A hot bath and early to bed had been on Pam's agenda—not unexpected visitors. Although she couldn't imagine who'd be dropping by unannounced to see her, anyway.

She peered through the peephole.

"Oh, my gosh!" She pulled open the door. "Sandy, what are you doing here?"

Her sister bounced into the house. "This is so *coool*, Sis. Immense! Mom said the guy you're living with had megabucks, but you know how she always exaggerates." A good thirty pounds overweight, Sandy wore a loosely fitting dress, and her light brown hair was tied back in an equally loose braid.

"I'm not exactly living with—" Pam swallowed the lie. "It's only temporary."

"Wow! Look at that tree! You know how much those things cost per foot? Man, this guy must be rolling in dough."

"Is there something wrong, Sandy? Why didn't you call before coming down? Are Mom and Dad okay? Your kids?"

"They're all fine. I just took a chance on catching you at home."

Her sister just *happened* to be in the neighborhood, some sixty miles from home, and decided to drop by? Something was definitely on her mind. Pam was almost afraid to ask.

"Come on in the TV room," she said. "You want some coffee? Something cold to drink?"

"No, that's okay." With little effort to disguise her curiosity, Sandy followed Pam through the house, gawking up the stairs and into the dining room.

Picking up the remote, Pam switched off the sitcom that hadn't been holding her attention anyway. She motioned for her sister to sit down.

"So, are you and this guy going to get married, Sis? Or just shack up for a while?"

"We haven't, ah . . ." At this point, Pam didn't have a clue as to what the future held. She'd tried not think about the fact that there had been no commitments asked for or given between her and Lucky. And her sister was one of the last people she wanted to discuss the topic with. "So, what really brings you so far from home?"

"Oh, you know, Dwayne had to quit his job a couple of months ago."

"Again?" As far as Pam could tell, Sandy's husband hadn't held any job for more than six months since they'd been married, nearly eight years ago.

"You know how these things go. The woman he was working for was a real witch. She came on to him and then forced him to resign when he wouldn't do what she wanted. I told him to file a sexual harassment suit, but he thought that would be a black mark on his record."

His record? It'd be hard to find an employment history that had more smudges than Dwayne's. "So he's been unemployed for two months?"

Sandy shrugged. "Closer to three now."

"I'm sorry. I'm afraid I'm in no position to hire—"

"Oh, I'm sure he'll find a new job. He always does. It just may take a while." Sandy stood and paced across the room where she studied Lucky's collection of CDs. "See, the thing is, the landlady is threatening to evict us. We're kinda behind on the rent."

"How far behind?"

"About three months?"

"Doesn't Dwayne get unemployment benefits?"

"Well, sure, but the kids have to eat, don't they? You've never had any children, so you don't have any idea how hard it is to keep food on the table."

"No, I don't." The bitter taste of envy coated Pam's throat at the unfairness that her sister had been blessed with two beautiful children—and seemed totally unable to cope with them—when she had been unable to conceive even one child. "You could get a job, Sandy. You're an intelligent woman—"

"Becky still needs me at home. Besides, you know how much trouble I have with my back."

Mentally, Pam rolled her eyes. Her sister had always had one excuse or another that kept her from working. A back injury that Pam suspected was more imagined than real. Allergies to dust. The short-sightedness of prospective employers.

She sighed. "So, what do you want from me?"

"Well, if you could just loan us a little to tide us over till Dwayne gets settled again. You know, a couple of months' worth of rent to get the landlady off our case. We'll pay it back."

"Like you did the last time?"

Sandy had the good sense to look embarrassed. "You'll get it all back, Sis. I promise. Dwayne just has to find himself, find the right niche where he can use his talents."

Sure. And dollar bills grow on avocado trees. "Right now I'm really tapped out. The clinic—"

"You could ask this guy you're living with. He probably wouldn't even blink at a couple of thou—"

Lucky walked into the room from the back of the house. The rain that had been threatening most of the day must have started because a few drops shone on his dark, curly hair.

"What wouldn't I blink at?" he asked. The picture of domestic attentiveness, he crossed the room and bent to kiss Pam on her cheek. He was wearing one of his Western shirts with silver piping, and a tiny sprig of holly peeked out from his pocket.

Pam flushed and suppressed an instant and heated reaction to his blatantly sexual innuendo. "Lucky, I want you to meet my sister, Sandy Piasakic. Lucky O'Toole."

"Hey, nice to meet you," Sandy said. Smiling, she offered her hand. "Some place you've got here. Guess you're doing okay in the money department to have this kind of a spread."

"I'm doing fine, thank you."

"I was just asking Pam if she could—"

"Sandy!" Shooting her sister a warning look, Pam came to her feet. She wasn't about to let Lucky get embroiled in the financial woes of her sibling. "You wait here and I'll go get what you want. My purse is upstairs."

"That's great, Sis. You won't be sorry."

Pam already was, but that didn't change the fact that her sister's family was about to be thrown out on the street. She couldn't let that happen to her niece and nephew, however much their father and mother might be irresponsible flakes. She loved them. It was as simple as that.

She was searching for her checkbook when Lucky knocked on the open door.

"You can tell me it's none of my business," he said.

Her hands stilled. "My sister and her husband have had some bad luck lately. He's out of work—"

"Not for the first time, I'd guess."

"Well, no, but—"

"The nuns at the orphanage were real good about teaching homilies. One that stuck in my head was something about 'Never a lender nor a borrower be.' Except for the mortgage on this place, I've pretty well tried to stick with that idea."

"You have no right to criticize me when you were so eager to give money to your friend who was down on his luck."

"You're right. But Howard had been good to me in the past, and I owed him. That doesn't mean I intend to support him for the rest of his life. I'm confident he'll get his act together. He needed a leg up, just the way he gave me one years ago."

"Sandy is my sister."

"That doesn't mean you have to be responsible for her."

"She has two children."

"Great. You want the kids to come live here with us, I wouldn't object. I just think adults ought to stand on their own two feet."

Pam stared down at the checkbook in her hand. Intellectually, she knew he was right. Emotionally, she couldn't bear the thought of being responsible for her sister and the children being evicted from their home. "How could I possibly tell her no?" she asked hopelessly.

"You'd be doing her a favor."

"I'll tell her this is absolutely the last time I'll bail her out. She'll simply have to get a job, or her husband will have to get his act together."

He cocked his eyebrow in disapproval. "If you do that, she'll be back. It'll be like a revolving door."

Stubbornly, Pam scribbled out the check. Maybe she was being softhearted, even *softheaded*. But Sandy was her sister. And Lucky had no right to tell her what to do.

She brushed past him to go back downstairs and wondered why on earth there were tears in her eyes. Her emotions had been so volatile the last couple of days she didn't quite know what to make of herself. At the clinic that morning she'd dropped a sample bottle of antibiotics, spilling the pills, and had burst into tears.

Now she seemed to be going out of her way to pick a fight with Lucky, when all she really wanted was to curl up in his arms.

PAM SLAMMED THE DRAWER shut so hard it shook the medical certificate hanging on the wall of the examining room. Leaving her patient and his mother behind, she stomped out into the hallway.

"Irma Sue!" she growled, her teeth clenched. "There are no surgical gloves in Room 2 and no needles. How am I supposed to stitch up that child's laceration without the proper equipment?"

The nurse's dark eyes widened. "Unless one of your little patients is playing tricks on you, the box of gloves is right where it always is—right on top of the counter."

"On top of the counter?" She'd looked on the counter. Hadn't she?

"Like always." Irma Sue planted her fist on her ample hip. "And them little pokey needles come in a new box now—an itty-bitty blue-and-white one. You were probably looking for the old kind."

"The old kind," Pam echoed. What the devil was the matter with her, yelling at Irma Sue?

"Now listen here, sister." Irma Sue backed her toward the office. "The last few days you've been as testy as a porcupine wearing his skin inside out. If I didn't know you better, I'd say you were suffering the all-time biggest case of PMS there ever was."

"Don't be silly. I—" Pam knew she'd been riding a fine edge since before Sandy showed up at her door looking for a handout. But PMS? Why, her last period had only been . . . weeks ago. Possibly five or six weeks ago.

Stunned disbelief hit Pam like a sledgehammer.

She was a doctor, for heaven's sake. Unintended pregnancies didn't happen to her. She was too smart, too knowledgeable about the human reproductive system to get caught in that sort of a trap.

But she and Lucky hadn't taken one single precaution to avoid pregnancy.

Their brains must have gone on vacation when their respective libidos had gotten loose.

Except Pam knew she *couldn't* get pregnant. Hadn't she and Ted tried for three long years? He'd even taken the initiative to have himself checked, a process that no man looked forward to with enthusiasm. And since he'd been declared one hundred percent normal, the fault must have been hers. Right?

She frowned. Of course, the current problem could be the emotional roller coaster she'd been riding the last few weeks, since Lucky showed up in her life—and in her bed. That would be enough to alter any woman's cycle.

"Dr. Pam, are you all right?"

Pam blinked and gave Irma Sue an apologetic smile. "You know, I'm not quite sure," she said thoughtfully.

But that evening as Pam was getting ready to go home, she noticed Dr. Ulrich's car in the hospital parking lot. He was the urologist Ted had consulted so many years ago.

On the basis of a disturbing hunch, Pam searched the doctor out on the medical floor.

"Hello, Wally, how have you been?" she said when she found him at the nurses' station making notations on a patient's chart. A heavy-set man, he had to stand at arm's length from the counter because his stomach was in the way.

"Ah, Dr. Pam, good to see you, my dear. Just another day in the medical factory, right? I trust you are getting along all right."

"Quite well, thank you." If you consider tense as a bowstring or blubbering with tears to be a healthy situation.

"No raging epidemics of chicken pox in the offing?"

"I hope not, though my patients usually save that particular disease for a Christmas Eve crisis."

"Umm," he said noncommittally as he continued to write a medication order on the chart. "I was thinking about your husband the other day. Fine man. Always a pity to lose a friend who is both a fellow doctor and a patient."

"Ted had the utmost confidence in you as a physician, Wally. In fact, because of your friendship, it must have been doubly difficult for you to tell him he wasn't likely to father any children of his own."

The doctor shifted his attention from the chart to Pam. "Actually, he said you and he had decided 'giving birth' to the clinic was far more important than having a family. Normally, it can be very stressful for a man to learn he is unable to produce children—procreation is so important to women—but at least this time you were both in agreement."

Agreement? The question nearly screamed from Pam's lungs. She had secretly cried herself to sleep for months because she'd thought the failure was *hers!* And Ted was being so patient and understanding.

What incredible cruelty had made Ted lie to her? Had it been male ego? Or had he been content all along for them not to have children when she had so desperately wanted a large family? Had he only been using her for his own needs, those that made their medical partnership more important than the union of a man and woman who wanted to create a family together?

Anger rocketed through her, followed quickly by a huge dose of disillusionment. The man had used her in the most heartless of ways. He had undermined her sense of self-worth, no less so than a husband who physically battered his wife. He'd taken her dream from her. In return, he'd substituted his own vision of happiness, one she didn't entirely share.

Like a pane of glass struck by a rock, the image of her picture-perfect marriage to Ted shattered into a thousand disjointed pieces. She should have listened to her inner voice that urged her to seek treatment from a fertility specialist. Instead, she had let herself be convinced by Ted that she was just under too much stress from starting the new clinic and that there would be more time for specialists and involved treatments after the clinic was up and running smoothly.

The wash of shame that swamped her provided the answer. She'd been too afraid to have his words confirmed, too terrified to know beyond doubt that she was something less than a whole woman.

But maybe, in fact, that wasn't the truth. At this very moment she could be carrying the child of a man to whom she wasn't married, and she had no real idea how he felt about her. At least as far as commitment was concerned.

A hysterical bubble of laughter—formed from a collection of hormones that were clearly on the fritz and a reaction to the fury she felt toward her former husband—threatened to explode from within her.

After telling Wally Urlich good-night, she made her way back to her car.

Life, it would seem, was decidedly unpredictable.

Chapter Eleven

Kneeling precariously on the open half door of Sweet Sigh's stall, Angie tried to lure the mare toward her with a carrot. Rainy days were boring, particularly when Lucky was in his office doing 'portant stuff, and Dr. Pam was talking on the phone to her mother.

"M'ere, horsey," she crooned. "'Member me? I'm your friend."

Sweet Sigh nudged Angie's palm with her big, soft lips. Moving her hand a little, Angie got the horse to take a step sideways, putting her in perfect position to be mounted.

Well, sort of perfect.

With a grunt, Angie launched herself across Sweet Sigh's back. The mare did a little dance, but Angie managed to hold on long enough to straddle the horse and grab her mane. She smiled. Getting on a horse wasn't so hard. But she was sure up high, higher than she'd ever been except for when Lucky had been holding her on that tall stepladder to put the little angel on top of the tree.

"Hey, what are you doing?" José yelled from the other side of the stall.

Darn it all. She'd thought José was busy in the tack room. "Go away. I'm learning to be a jockey."

"You're too little to be a jockey. Besides, Lucky will kill you if you hurt his best racer."

"I'm not gonna hurt anything. Sweet Sigh likes me."

"Hey, if she spooks she's likely to jam her leg, or somethin'. You'd better get off or I'm telling my grandpa."

"Oh, you're no fun." Angie laid her head down on Sweet Sigh's neck and petted her. She loved the smell of the horse, her smooth coat and the silky feel of her mane. As far as Angie was concerned, horses were the best animals in the whole, wide world. Better 'n dogs and cats, or even lions and tigers.

"I'm tellin' on you right now, and when Lucky finds out what you've been doing, he's gonna send you away."

She glowered at her friend. "You just wait, José. Some day I'm gonna be a jockey and make lots and lots of money. Then you'll be sorry you tattled on me."

"Yeah, sure. You can tell that to Lucky when he's driving you to the county home for bratty little kids."

"I'm not bratty," she cried. Least ways, she didn't mean to be.

When José turned to go find Rafael, Angie panicked. Getting tattled on would get her in big trouble, even if she hadn't hurt anything. She slid off the horse and scampered beneath the chain that kept Sweet Sigh from wandering around inside the horse barn.

"You don't have to go tell nobody. See? I'm off."

José eyed her suspiciously. "You better stay off, too, if you know what's good for you."

Angie jammed her fists in her jeans pockets and sighed. She really did wish she had a horse of her very own. That way she could sit on top of it anytime she wanted and go for rides, too.

Walking outside, she saw a police car drive up to the house. It was that policeman with the big mustache who'd asked her so many questions at the hospital. She didn't much like him.

Angie didn't think José had told on her—yet. But she figured she'd better find somethin' to do in the barn. Somethin' *good,* like sweeping the floor.

LUCKY LOOKED UP from his accounting ledger when the doorbell rang. He'd been working on the payroll and Christmas bonuses for his employees. It had been a good year. He figured he could be generous.

Setting aside his pen, he headed for the front door.

As he passed the stairway, he looked up toward Pam's room. She'd been as edgy as a mare about to come into heat the last few days. One minute affectionate, the next as bristly as a two-day old beard. He guessed he should have kept his mouth shut about her loaning money to her sister. Maybe he didn't know enough about families to understand why she'd give away her hard-earned money to someone so clearly irresponsible—particularly a woman who had tried to cozy up to him the first time they'd met. Hell, Pam had hardly been out of sight when Sandy had hit him up for a loan.

It had made him sick to his stomach.

Money attracted a lot of scavengers, if you let it. Lucky had learned to be on guard. Maybe Pam hadn't caught on to that lesson yet. Or maybe she had too generous a heart.

He grinned. A man could do worse than being on the receiving end with a woman like that, even if she often disguised the depth of her emotions. She was like a crusty marshmallow—a little tough on the outside with an extraordinarily soft core. Tasty, too, he mused.

Opening the door, he was surprised to find the Meadowbrook Police Chief standing on his porch shaking rain from his hat.

"Somebody call the cops?" Lucky asked, raising his eyebrows.

"Nope. But I've got some news I think you'll want to hear. The doctor, too, if she's here."

Fear twisted through Lucky's gut like a six-inch blade. My God, they'd found Angie's parents! He was going to lose her... and Pam.

He braced himself in response to the painful blow. "Come on in, Chief. I'll call Pam. She's upstairs."

PAM RESPONDED TO Lucky's call by swinging her legs over the side of the bed and sitting up. Her eyes felt gluey, her limbs strangely heavy. Never in her life had she felt so lacking in energy. Of course, any telephone conversation with her mother drained her. Learning her brother was having a wonderful time in Florida living on the beach hadn't helped, or the fact that her sister's husband had taken a few days off from job hunting to attend a class in metaphysical hoopla.

Maybe she shouldn't throw stones at poor, incompetent Dwayne, she considered as she ran her fingers through her hair and headed downstairs. Recently she'd been doing a fine job of procrastinating herself. She'd purchased a pregnancy kit yesterday—at a drugstore where no one knew her. It was still sitting on the bathroom counter. Mocking her. To determine the most likely reason for her fatigue and erratic emotions, all she had to do was take the damn test.

She gritted her teeth.

Somewhere along the way, she must have learned not to ask a question when she wasn't prepared to deal with the answer.

She found Lucky in the living room standing by the fireplace looking decidedly uncomfortable. Chief Coleman appeared equally ill at ease. Anxiety prickled along the length of her spine. She had the disturbing feeling an unintended pregnancy was going to be the least of her worries this weekend.

She greeted Larry with a nod. "Is there something wrong?" she asked.

"Well, now, I personally don't know what to make of it, but we got a lead on Angie's past."

"Her parents?"

Lucky took her hand, tugging her toward him, feeling pretty darn sure whatever news the chief had wouldn't be good.

"Through the FBI, we've located the last foster home where Angie lived," Coleman said. He continued to fiddle self-consciously with his hat.

"Oh?" Pam smiled. "That should at least help us find her current guardians."

Switching his attention from his hat, the officer fussed with his big mustache, smoothing the curved tips on either side of his mouth. "Turns out it's kind of a dead end, if you'll excuse the pun, doctor."

Pam shot Lucky a puzzled look. "I don't understand."

"I'm not sure I do, either." But he didn't like Coleman's troubled expression or his uneasy gestures.

"We've checked her fingerprints," the chief explained. "A lot of families, including foster families, have their kids fingerprinted in case the youngster is kidnapped, gets lost, you know." He shrugged. "Well, they came up with a match for Angie."

Pam nodded. "That's good."

"It turns out Angie's fingerprints match those of a child by the same name who died in a house fire in Bismarck, North Dakota about six weeks ago. One of those space heater fires the first cold night of the year."

Sinking down to sit on the arm of the couch, Pam said, "But that's not possible."

Lucky silently agreed. In spades! But he had an equally sinking feeling that what the police chief was telling them was true.

"It's not possible in any case I've heard about," Coleman grumbled. "Doesn't make a nickel's worth of sense to me, but that's what the report says. Thought I had to pass it on."

Leaving Pam's side for the moment, knowing he had to get rid of the police chief as quickly as possible, Lucky rested his hand on Coleman's shoulder in a jovial, one-of-the-boys way. He could see Pam was shaken by the officer's announcement, just as he was. She looked so pale he knew he had to give her time to adjust to the bizarre possibility he was fast reconsidering—that what Angie had tried to explain to him right after the accident was true. Her words about Saint Peter and finding new parents hadn't made a damn bit of sense...until now.

"You know how bureaucracies make mistakes, Larry," Lucky said. "This wouldn't be the first time somebody screwed up. But we appreciate you dropping by. If you hear anything else, you'll let us know, won't you?"

"Sure." He placed his hat back on his head. "I just thought you ought to know."

Lucky ushered the police chief toward the front door. "You did the right thing. I bet as a police officer you could write a book about the goofs those bureaucrats make. It's only us poor slobs down here in the trenches who have any idea what's really going on."

"You've got that right, Mr. O'Toole. I appreciate your understanding." He glanced out the open door at the continuing downpour of rain. "Lord, I sure do hope this rain lets up soon. Last rainy season we had the banks of every creek in the county overflowing.

Wouldn't want to go through that again. Whole areas were stranded and a half-dozen folks drowned."

"Yeah, I remember. All the power lines were down, too."

The chief stepped outside with a promise to keep looking for Angie's parents, then dashed through the rain toward his car.

Lucky blew out a long breath as he closed the door. From the way his heart was beating, he felt as if he'd just scored on a fifty-to-one shot that crossed the finish line first. A crazy feeling.

Back in the living room, he found Pam still sitting on the end of the couch, her arms wrapped around herself. He sat down next to her and tugged her into his lap. She came willingly enough, a sure sign of her emotional turmoil.

"How awful," she whispered. "A child dying in a house fire. Such a waste of a young life."

"Yeah." He brushed a kiss to her forehead. She smelled sweet and sexy, and this was the wrong time to be thinking about that.

"Of course, it must be a mistake," she said. She rested her head on his shoulder. "Our Angie couldn't be—"

"Remember when we first met in the emergency room?"

She nodded.

"Angie had been giving me some cockamamy story about dying too soon—you know, before her time—and then having a chance to pick us as parents."

"She had a mild concussion. Being a little disoriented—"

"I think we should talk to her."

She pulled back from him, her eyes wide. "You don't believe—"

"There are a lot of things in this world I don't understand, sweetheart. Hell, I don't even understand how I can turn on the TV and see moving pictures inside that little box. But that doesn't mean they aren't there." He ran the back of his knuckles down the softness of her cheek. God, she felt good. All of her. One of the most astounding things was how much he wanted her to want him. Forever. And it scared him to death. "Let's talk to Angie."

ANGIE WAS SO LITTLE, when she scooted back onto the couch, her legs stuck straight out.

"You don't believe me, do you?" she asked, her gaze riveted on her muddy, red tennis shoes.

Pam sat on the coffee table in front of the child with her hand resting on Angie's thigh. She'd been sitting there while she'd listened to the most incredible tale imaginable. Lucky sat next to the child, his arm around her narrow shoulders.

"I know sometimes children have wonderful imaginations," Pam said, keeping her voice calm and unaccusing. "They can make up wild stories that aren't really lies, but aren't quite the truth, either. Is this one of those times, honey?"

She gazed at Pam solemnly. "Nuh-uh. Saint Peter couldn't find my name in his big book so he said I could come back down to earth till I'm s'posed to die."

"And you picked me and Lucky to live with."

Nodding, Angie said, "I used to get real sick. I had asthma real bad, and once I gots ammonia. I thought you'd be able to fix me if I got sick again."

"I'd certainly try," Pam agreed, inwardly smiling at Angie's mispronunciation of "pneumonia." She'd suspected all along Angie had a history of chronic illness, but the thought that the child had actually died and returned to earth was totally outside her experience or understanding.

"What about me, sport? How come you picked me to be your old man?"

Angie failed to meet his gaze. "I can't tell you. Saint Peter said I wasn't s'posed to be greedy."

Chuckling, Lucky hugged her. "That's okay, kid. At least you're more honest than most women I've met."

Pam patted the child's leg. "Why don't you go upstairs and clean up? Maybe we can get Lucky to take us out to lunch."

"For a hamburger?" she asked, brightening.

"You got it, sport."

Scrambling off the couch, Angie ran out of the room, then came to an abrupt halt. At the doorway she turned. "I sure hope you two decide before Christmas that it's okay for me to stay. 'Cause I love you both bunches and bunches."

Pam's heart constricted so fiercely that for a moment she couldn't draw a breath. For so many years she'd wanted nothing more than to have a child to love, she'd had no idea how much that act would also have the power to bring her pain. Angie belonged with Lucky. That had been obvious from the beginning. Pam was an addendum, an afterthought, necessary only so that government authorities would approve of him acting as the child's guardian.

Standing, Pam paced across the room to stand by Angie's *gihugeic* Christmas tree and look out at the rain drenching the nearby pastures and the hillside across the canyon. She could hear the happy echo of the child's excited laughter the night they had all decorated the tree, and the press of tears burned at the back of her eyes.

She had no idea if she was included in Lucky's long-term plans—or if there was room in his heart for the baby she felt sure she was carrying.

He came up behind her and slipped his arms around her, resting his big, strong hands on her midsection...above his child. His breath was warm and sweetly scented.

"What do you think?" he asked.

She rested her hands on his far larger ones, hands she had learned were both gentle and arousing. "I think Angie believes every word she said."

"But you don't."

"I've been trained as a medical doctor and a scientist. To believe her story requires a huge leap of faith."

"A little dose of faith now and then probably never hurt anyone."

"The question remains, what are we going to do about Angie?" What are we going to do about *us?* she wanted to ask. The *four* of us.

"What's to do? I'm perfectly happy with things the way they are now. She can stay here with me forever, as far as I'm concerned." Nuzzling her neck, he placed a soft kiss at the juncture of her shoulder. "So can you, Doc. As long as you'd like."

An aching sense of longing filled her chest. Perversely, she'd hoped for his declaration of love. His acknowledgement that, in spite of their obvious differences, they could all be a family—a family to which they could add their own babies.

But he hadn't said the words, the same words, she realized, that Ted had spoken glibly and then betrayed.

Dear heaven, what was she to believe?

In her heart, she knew that without Lucky's love, she'd have to go on pretending that all she wanted was an uncommitted relationship. Like her father, she had never been a very skilled actor. Yet could she ever again have confidence in her own feelings, much less those of an Irish rogue who'd built his entire life on finding a two-dollar winning ticket at the races?

Lucky pulled Pam more tightly against him, inhaling deeply of her fresh, sweet scent. His body tightened even as his heart grew heavy.

Rejection was a hard thing to deal with. But he'd learned as a kid not to expect much. And he'd sure as hell heard Pam's silent message. If she didn't want him on a permanent basis, he could handle that. He'd take it one day at a time. And maybe he'd crank up some of that faith the nuns had tried teaching him. Miracles did happen. And if Angie was right, Saint Peter would be on his side.

"Hey, it's too bad I promised burgers to Angie," he said, his need thickening hoarsely in his throat. He found Pam's earlobe and nibbled lightly. "I can think of an alternate way to spend a rainy afternoon that would be pretty terrific."

The audible catch of her breath and the slight tremble of her shoulders suggested she had an interest in the same sort of diversion.

"The joys of parenthood," she said dryly as she slipped from his grasp. "I'll go get my rain jacket."

ANGIE RESTED HER ELBOWS on the windowsill and plopped her chin on her fists.

"Mister Saint Peter, are you still around?"

"Of course, Angelica. Is there a problem?"

"Well, see, I told Lucky and Dr. Pam the truth— about me and how I burned up and stuff, and how you said I could come back. But I don't think they believed me."

"Humans have some difficulty believing what they can't see."

"I can't see you."

"But you did once, didn't you?"

She sighed. It seemed like such a long time ago, Angie wasn't sure anymore. Her chin trembled. "I sure wish they'd decide pretty soon that I could be their little girl. It's gettin' awful close to Christmas."

"I know, Angelica, and I'm doing the very best I can for you. But humans appear to have developed a stubborn streak that is far more recalcitrant than... Well, let us simply say, they do like to enjoy the exercise of free choice."

BY MONDAY NIGHT, Pam realized that not only were her hormones in wild disarray, she was also incredibly behind in her Christmas shopping. There was almost no time left and she still had to buy presents for Irma Sue and her family, plus her own parents, her niece and nephew, Angie and Lucky. The only bright spot was that some months ago she'd ordered rather generic presents for all the hospital nurses on the pediatric floor.

With a sense of desperation, she plowed through the crowds at the mall. This procrastination wasn't like her at all. Normally right after Thanksgiving she purchased all of her Christmas gifts, and most of them were quickly wrapped and stored neatly in piles ready for delivery to the appropriate recipients.

But it had been shortly after Thanksgiving that Angie and Lucky showed up in the emergency room. Clearly, they'd been a very unsettling experience in her usually well-ordered life.

Arms laden with presents, Pam shoved open the front door to Lucky's house... her home, however temporarily.

Lucky met her in the entryway, a portable phone in his hand. "Good timing. It's your brother. He called collect." He extended the instrument.

She dumped her packages on the floor. "No peeking," she warned.

Lucky gave her one of those innocent Who-me? looks that she didn't buy for a minute. She draped her coat over the pile before she took the phone.

"Reggie? How's it going?"

"Great, Sis, really great. We've had a couple of terrific gigs. Got a standing ovation one night. Sure gets the adrenaline flowing. It was really cool."

"That's wonderful, but I was sorry you left school before the quarter was over. I'd hoped—"

"Yeah, I know. And the fact is, I'm not sure this trip was all that good an idea."

Static crackled on the long distance line. "Why is that, Reggie?" she asked suspiciously.

"Well, see, our agent kinda ripped us off."

Pam didn't like the sound of that. "What do you mean?"

"The guy took our money and split. He was a real flake." She heard a deep sigh on the other end of the line. "We're busted, Sis. Flat broke. We're sleeping out on the beach. Heck, we don't even have money to buy gas to get home."

It could be cold even in Florida this time of year. Pam knew that. But she made the mistake of looking up and catching Lucky's eye. Guilt at helping out too much crowded in around her chest. "That's too bad, Reggie. But you and your friends are big boys. I'm sure you can figure out something."

"Come on, Sis. We need your help. Just a couple of hundred bucks. We can't get home. I'll be back in school after the Christmas break, I promise. I know I can make up my exams. No big deal.''

Pam's hand slid across her midsection. She had someone else to think about now besides herself, a child that was entirely her responsibility. She couldn't rely on Lucky's largesse to keep her clinic going any more than Reggie should be relying on her for his upkeep. At some point, she needed to draw a line in the sand. The Florida beach sand was as good a place as any to start. At least her brother would be unlikely to freeze.

''Aren't there four of you in your combo?'' she asked.

''Yeah, but—''

''I think among you there ought to be ways to land a few jobs. How 'bout becoming waiters? Or parking valets? I'm sure there's a way—''

''Pammy, what are you talking about?'' her brother asked hysterically. ''I wanna come home. We don't even have a place to sleep. You've got to—''

She focused on O'Toole's bright blue eyes and steeled herself against habits that had been ingrained since she'd been ten years old. Reggie was *not* her responsibility. If he was old enough to make decisions, he was old enough to accept the consequences of those decisions. ''I'm sure you'll find a way to do what you need to, Reggie. Keep me posted.'' Deliberately, her heart thudding against her ribs, she severed the connection.

Lucky cocked her a half smile. ''You're one hell of a smart lady, Doc, and you learn real quick. I'm impressed.''

"Impressed that I've just left my little brother stranded in Florida with no way to get home? I'm having a fair number of second thoughts right about now, but thanks for your vote of confidence."

He tunneled his fingers through her hair. "I'm impressed enough so I think you deserve a kiss of congratulations. What you just did couldn't have been easy for you."

No, it hadn't been.

But the warmth of his lips eased some of her concern. She knew he'd made it on his own as a boy of fourteen. Surely her brother, older by several years, would be able to manage as well.

Allowing the kiss to deepen, her tongue teased with his until the fusing of their mouths became more intense and passion stirred with familiar ardor. He knew exactly how to arouse her. As though they were two parts of the same puzzle, she felt herself melting into him.

The scent of Christmas holly and fragrant candle wax filled the air, and the feeling of celebration crowded into Pam's heart. For tonight, she wanted to believe that all of her tomorrows would be spent in Lucky's arms.

His breathing raspy, Lucky whispered, "If we don't slow down, we'll never make it upstairs."

"Is Angie asleep?"

"Yeah. She went to bed more than an hour ago."

The uninhibited thrill of pursuing the forbidden shivered through Pam. "Have you ever done it in front of a Christmas tree?"

His eyes darkened to indigo beneath half-lowered lids. "I'm game if you are."

Emotion tightened her throat. "Yes." She wanted to be wild; she wanted to be tender. She wanted to experience every possible feeling with Lucky—to taste his salty flavor, catch his musky scent, test the corded strength of his body.

In the living room, the lights winked in a brilliant rainbow of colors. As they discarded their clothes, Pam explored with her hands the treasures revealed by each spectrum of light. Winking reds illuminated Lucky's chest and the swirls of dark hair that sprang against her palms, the pads of muscles she kneaded with her fingertips. She lingered momentarily to taste his nipples, drawing a soft groan from him and making his muscles tense beneath her fingers.

"Ah, Doc, you've been hiding your talents."

"I've been learning from a good teacher."

The blue lights reflected in his eyes, sparkling like multifaceted gems worth more than any pot of gold at the end of a rainbow.

Intimately, she surveyed his arousal with her fingertips, then cupped his taut flesh gently with both hands.

She smiled and whispered, *"Gihugeic."*

A deep sound vibrated in Lucky's chest that could have been a laugh, or a far more elemental response.

He drew her down to the plush carpeting and the flickering greens and golds of the tree became as wildly enchanting as comets, burning as hot as the sun. She flexed her fingers into his hard muscles, lightly scored his shoulders with her nails.

"I want you, Lucky. All of you."

He refused to grant her wish immediately. "First, I want to pleasure you."

She arched up to him. "I don't think I can wait."

"Waiting can be its own reward."

She opened her mouth to protest any delay but he silenced her with a deep kiss that made her moan. His tongue parried with hers in a slow dance while his hand caressed her hot flesh with unhurried strokes. The shocking pleasure of his sensual touch ignited a flame that threatened to become incandescent. Heat spiraled through her in glittering waves.

Her breath broke on a sob. "Lucky—"

"Is something wrong?" he teased.

"Yes...no...you're not...playing fair." She couldn't talk, she couldn't think. All she could do was feel. His tongue. His lips. The rough calluses on hands that gentled and coaxed her with such tenderness that she had no will of her own.

Tension built and throbbed within her, sending her climbing a river of color beyond the rainbow. He entered her and the blue of the sky was within her reach, the gold of the sun, the midnight black of all the shades of the universe mixing together in a zenith of perfection.

In a transforming moment, like the miracle of dawn bursting through the night, Pam was transported to a paradise she had never known or dreamed about.

Chapter Twelve

Pam stood in the center of her clinic's waiting room late the next afternoon. It was empty now after another day of nonstop patients. This had been Ted's dream, she realized. *His baby.* The choice of pictures on the walls, the carpeting, even the furnishings had been based on his taste, not hers. She'd simply gone along, so filled with respect—perhaps even awe—for her new husband, she'd been happy to defer to his wishes. So anxious for security she hadn't wanted to rock the boat.

From a very young age she'd wanted to be a doctor. As she went through med school, she grew increasingly certain she wanted to be a pediatrician. But she'd had another dream to go along with that. One her husband had apparently not shared.

Children. A chance for her to be a mother and Ted a father.

She'd been devastated to think she couldn't conceive his child. But there were alternatives like adoption or utilizing donor eggs, which he wouldn't even consider. He had told her they should wait awhile—until the clinic was on its feet, until they were a little more settled, until... until... it was too late.

What a shattering series of self-serving lies he had told her.

As she walked toward the back of the office, she smiled at the arrangement of Christmas holly on the reception desk. Lucky certainly knew how to keep himself right up front in her awareness. Her footsteps hesitated by the storeroom and she felt the warm glow of memories. No matter how he felt about her, whether or not there was any hope for them to have a long-term relationship, what she was about to start in motion now was the right thing to do. For her. And for her child.

In her mind she pictured a chubby-cheeked baby with bright blue eyes, a devil-may-care smile, and wavy, raven hair. Even without the pregnancy test that still sat on the bathroom counter, Pam knew that within her womb a new life had begun. Every passing day without her period confirmed that belief.

Retrieving her purse from the office, she locked up and headed across the street to the hospital for her appointment with the administrator. The rain had let up for now but it was still cold and damp.

She met Roger Peltam at the front door and they went up in the elevator together to the second floor administrative offices.

"What's this all about, Dr. Pam?" he asked, his voice booming in the close confines of the elevator. He slid his hand across the door when it opened so she could step out first.

"I'm about to make some changes as far as the clinic is concerned. As one of Meadowbrook's leading citizens, I thought you'd like to know so you and others can make appropriate plans."

He slanted her a puzzled look.

The hospital administrator's secretary had gone for the day but Arnold Thacher's office door stood ajar. Pam knocked and went inside.

"Ah, there you are, Dr. Pam. Roger. Come in."

Arnold stood, motioning them to the leather chairs in front of his walnut desk where only a yellow notepad and a single pen marred the empty expanse. In contrast, Pam's desk was a jumble of medical journals and patient records. She wondered how on earth the man could manage a hospital this large without a stack of paper ten feet high covering every available horizontal space in his office. But maybe that was why he was an administrator and Pam was more comfortable in the role of physician.

"Now, then, Dr. Pam..." Seated again in his swivel chair, Arnold leaned back and tented his fingers in front of his markedly narrow lips. "What can I do for you?"

"I've reached a decision that I wanted to discuss with both you and Roger before I take the next step. I believe I'm more than a competent pediatric physician, but the burden of administering the clinic and trying to run it as a solo practice has become too much for me."

"You're taking on a partner?" Roger asked.

"I've considered that possibility. My preference would be to sell the clinic outright."

Arnold's receding hairline slipped down into a frown. "We've had a very close relationship with your clinic, Dr. Pam. Certainly, your medical practice has contributed in a positive way to our occupancy rate. I would hope whoever purchases the clinic—"

"Ideally, Arnold, I believe the pediatric clinic should be an integral part of the hospital, wholly owned and operated by the same corporation. Naturally, I'd be happy to stay on as a staff physician." Working far fewer hours than her current twelve to fourteen a day. Motherhood, she happily thought, was going to take up a great deal of her time. And if by some odd quirk of fate she wasn't pregnant, simply having a little fun was high on her agenda. That thought was a very liberating one.

The administrator's eyes narrowed, and she could almost see the mental calculations spinning through his mind. "Pediatric clinics are not normally good profit centers for a hospital. Often, they are loss leaders, so to speak."

"That's why I wanted Roger here." She turned to the man next to her. "I believe Meadowbrook needs a pediatric clinic. It's crucial to the well-being of any community that its children have good medical care. I would think, as an ongoing charitable effort, the Rotary might want to take responsibility for underwriting some of the expenses."

"Oh, I don't know..." Frowning, Roger shook his head. "That would be a very large project."

"And popular in town," she added. "Raising funds for the clinic would most likely garner considerable respect for any organization within the community."

"Well, yes, I suppose it would be a positive activity. But—"

"Of course, I thought of the Rotary first, and you, Roger. My second choice would be the Kiwanis." Roger's head snapped up, as Pam had known it would. "That group seems to be gaining a good deal of influence within the community. Of course, the Lions Club is a possibility, too."

Roger cleared his throat. "I'll have to talk with the board members, but I think the Rotary can handle the job."

"The Rotary might even consider leading a joint effort among all the service clubs," she suggested.

Beaming, Arnold agreed. "Given sufficient assurances of future underwriting, I'm sure the hospital would be glad to take the clinic under our administrative wing."

"I do want to make sure my existing staff is guaranteed continuing employment at the same level of pay and benefits, or higher, of course."

"I'm sure that can be arranged," Arnold promised.

A weight lifted from Pam's shoulders and she breathed more easily than she had in years. She hadn't realized how heavy a burden the clinic had become. Or how difficult the memories of her late husband had grown. She needed to shed both impediments in order to get on with her life.

Strange. Hadn't Lucky said something much like that shortly after they met? How in heaven's name had he been so perceptive from the very beginning?

Pam stopped off at her town house to pick up her dress for the party that evening before going home to Lucky's. Excitement fluttered through her midsection as she selected black lace undies and a garter belt. Amazingly, this would be her first actual date with Lucky. She intended to make it a memorable one.

Later that evening, she dressed carefully, inserting tiny diamond studs in her ears, the one extravagant gift Ted had given her as a wedding present. He'd been far happier spending his money on state-of-the-art medical equipment for the clinic.

As she checked her appearance in the mirror, she saw Angie peering in through the bedroom door, her eyes wide.

"What do you think?" Pam asked.

"I think you must be the prettiest lady in the whole world."

Pam laughed. "I'm not sure about that but thank you."

"Lucky's gonna think you're gor-jeus!"

Lucky's reflection joined Angie's in the mirror. "She's right." His words of praise were low and rough with appreciation.

Turning, Pam intentionally set the full skirt of her otherwise skintight cocktail dress swirling. It was possible, like Angie, she'd put on a couple of pounds since she'd moved in with Lucky. The fabric clung tightly to every inch of her upper body until it flared below her hips.

"Thank you, kind sir." She smiled at him as he entered the room.

"Angie told me I had to give you flowers. It's what men do when they 'want to get it on.'" An amused smile teasing at the corners of his lips, he extended a corsage box toward her. "I figure she must know what she's talking about. She had it on the best authority— José."

"I see." Repressing a laugh, she opened the lid to the box. Cushioned by tissue paper was a wrist corsage of an unusual arrangement. Two spectacularly large orchids nestled in a bed of Christmas holly. Pam choked. "Where did you find a florist who would do this?"

"Money talks," he said smugly.

THE POSH HOTEL for the banquet was up the coast from the Del Mar racetrack and right on the ocean. The evening mist carried the heavy of trace of salt through the air.

As Pam slid into Lucky's arms for their first dance, she decided he might be a man who was a little rough around the edges, but he certainly looked good in a tux—a unique combination like exotic orchids and garden variety holly. The dark jacket emphasized his broad shoulders and flat stomach; the razor-edge crease in his pants accentuated his long legs. Pulling her close, he maneuvered them around the floor in a slow dance that demonstrated his easy, masculine grace. She followed him easily, as though they had been dancing together for years.

"You smell good," he said, his lips close to her ear, his voice low and intimate.

"So do you." Spicy and sexy and one hundred percent male.

"Amazing what can happen to a stable hand when you get him away from a barn."

"You haven't been a stable hand for a very long time."

"That's still where I feel the most comfortable. Getting all gussied up like this makes me feel like I'm a fraud."

"Your friends don't think you are." In fact, any number of the other guests at the benefit had stopped by their dinner table to sing his praises. It was clear the members of the Association of Racehorse Owners viewed Lucky as their natural leader. They deferred to his judgment, courted his approval and sought his friendship. He'd achieved his success, both personally and professionally, on his own, Pam realized. Few men could claim as much.

She wondered why she hadn't recognized the full range of Lucky's wonderful qualities from the beginning. Obviously she'd been blinded by her own prejudices. Only when she'd allowed her heart to have a serious conversation with her brain had her vision cleared. Or perhaps, if she were to believe Angie's story, Saint Peter had had a hand in helping her see the truth.

"Do we have to stay much longer?" she asked. The lights had been dimmed after the banquet meal and speeches had been completed. Now, with the band creating a romantic mood, the hall was filled with intimate shadows.

"You planning to turn into a pumpkin at the stroke of midnight?"

"No, but I've thought of an interesting way for us to end the evening."

"Um, sounds encouraging." He brushed a light kiss across the sensitive shell of her ear. "Tell me what you have in mind."

Swaying with the music, she pressed her pelvis suggestively into the nest of his hips. "I think I'd rather show you."

"Now that's an offer no man could resist."

IN SPITE OF the late night Lucky and Pam had enjoyed, first at the banquet and then in a mutual exploration of sexual intimacy, he woke early, as excited as a kid who could hardly wait one more day for Christmas to arrive. He slipped out of bed and Pam sighed, a sweet sound that almost drove him back beneath the covers. If he rejoined her, they'd be there for another hour. Maybe more. And he was pretty sure he'd heard Angie already up and moving.

Pam curled toward the warm sheets he had just vacated, the unconscious search for him pleasing Lucky no end. She'd been particularly passionate last night. He hoped that was a good sign she'd accept the extravagant Christmas gift he'd purchased for her, a little item he planned to give her tonight at the stroke of midnight.

Pulling on his jeans, he bolstered his courage. At least he was confident Angie would be pleased with her gift. Rafael was scheduled to pick up a sweet little mare after dark tonight and trailer her back to the farm. The red bow to tie around her neck was already waiting in the horse barn.

Downstairs, he put on the coffee. There was no sign of Angie. Some mornings she went out to visit the horses first thing. Or maybe he hadn't heard her get up after all, and he could have taken advantage of a lingering lovemaking session with Pam.

Resting his hands on the counter, he peered outside as he waited for the coffee to drip. It had rained again during the night and the sky was still heavily overcast. The weatherman was predicting a sloppy track for the holiday weekend. Unfortunately, not many of his horses were good mudders. He could only hope none of those horses racing would get injured, and was grateful he'd decided to scratch Sweet Sigh from the rest of the winter season, letting her rest up for the spring events that would lead to the Kentucky Derby.

He knew he'd made a name for himself on the West Coast as a racehorse owner. Perversely, he wanted more. The years he'd spent mucking stalls galled him— all the times some owner or hotshot trainer had called him "boy" still rankled. The kid who'd been kicked around wanted to show them he could make it to the big time. The Derby would give him that chance.

With only idle interest, his thoughts already split between Pam upstairs in his bed and what the day at the races would bring, he watched Angie ride out of the horse barn. Bareback.

On Sweet Sigh!

Realization shot through him with terrifying speed. What the hell?

He raced for the back door, leaped over the railing on the porch and ran after the horse and rider. Where the hell was Rafael? Or José? Why hadn't someone stopped her?

"Angie!" he shouted. "Come back!"

Either she didn't hear him because she'd already trotted too far down the driveway toward the road, or she couldn't turn the horse. Sweet Sigh could be damn obstinate when she wanted to be. Impossible to manage by anyone other than a trained rider.

"Rafael!" he shouted over his shoulder. "Get your butt out here!"

So far as Lucky knew, Angie had never even been on a horse. And she sure didn't have the strength to control the animal if she spooked.

As it was, the kid was bouncing up and down on the horse's back like a rubber ball, barely hanging on to her flowing mane. Angie was going to fall. No way could she keep her seat at that bumpy gait. She'd be better off if she kicked the horse into a smooth gallop. But then, Lucky would never catch up with them.

Horse and rider turned onto the road. Sweet Sigh wouldn't be able to go far on the asphalt without injury to her hooves. Her shoes were meant for grass or dirt, not a hard-surfaced pavement.

Lucky's lungs were beginning to burn; his leg muscles yelped at the unfamiliar strain. Damn, he was out of shape.

"Angie! Stop! Pull on the reins!"

She glanced over her shoulder. Her mouth formed a frightened O and her eyes were wide.

Just then a car rounded a bend in the road. Brakes squealed. Startled, Sweet Sigh veered across the road in front of the car. Angie screamed. Lucky's heart nearly stopped beating.

PAM SAT BOLT upright in bed.

It was like those days as an intern struggling to catch a catnap during a thirty-six hour shift when she'd come instantly awake to meet the next emergency.

But where was the emergency now?

Lucky was gone from the bed and his pillow was cold. She hadn't heard him get up.

Had she sensed that he was in trouble? Or was it Angie who needed her?

She pulled her robe on against the damp chill in the air and went to the window.

"Oh, my God . . ."

A car sat sideways across the road below the house, Sweet Sigh was standing in the gully beside the road, and Lucky—his black hair damp with the misting rain—knelt on the grassy verge next to a tiny body. Rafael and José were running down the driveway toward the accident.

Instincts honed by a thousand emergencies took over. Pam didn't think about Angie. She didn't dare. In-

stead, she simply reacted based on her years of training. Panic might come later. Even grief. But for now,
she was a doctor. She'd do what she'd been trained to
do.

Dressing hurriedly, she snatched up her cell phone
and punched in 911 as she ran down the stairs. She gave
the operator directions to Lucky's house. This far out
of town it might take fifteen minutes or longer for
paramedics to reach the location.

As she picked up the medical bag that she always left
by the front door, Pam prayed it contained whatever
emergency supplies might be necessary.

Approaching the scene, she noted Angie appeared
conscious and responsive, though she looked under-
standably frightened. Pam touched Lucky's shoulder as
she knelt on the opposite side of the child.

"I'll take a look," she said with a calmness she didn't
entirely feel.

A man standing beside the car, presumably the driver,
said, "I'm sorry, lady. Geez, the horse ran right in front
of me. I tried to stop. The kid—"

Ignoring the driver's comments, Lucky sat back on
his haunches. "I tried to keep her still. I was afraid..."
His voice cracked.

"Where does it hurt, honey?" she asked Angie,
knowing every one of the fears Lucky was experiencing
and sharing them with equal terror she was too well
trained to show. It was all she could do to suppress the
instinctive rush of motherly concern in favor of her
medical training. Never had she felt this way about any
other child—the tormenting wish that she could take the

pain on her own shoulders instead of letting the child suffer. In the last few weeks, without even having become aware of it happening, Pam had become Angie's mother, in her heart if not in fact.

"I think I hit my elbow." Angie held up her injured arm, bending it easily—a good sign that it wasn't broken in spite of the visible abrasion.

"How about your head? Did you hit it?"

"I don't think so." A frown stitched itself across her forehead. "But I landed real hard."

"I'm sure you did." The mirror of that blow struck Pam's midsection, momentarily stealing her breath. "Did you get the wind knocked out of you?"

She nodded solemnly. "I shouldn't have rode the horse, Dr. Pam. José told me—"

From the gully where Sweet Sigh was moving restlessly, Rafael called, "Lucky, I think you had better come take a look."

Knowing she had things under control with Angie, Pam indicated Lucky was free to see why his foreman needed him. With her eyes, she followed his progress down into the shallow gully, and what she saw made her sick to her stomach. Along Sweet Sigh's right foreleg lay a gash about eight inches long, deep enough so that not only the flesh but muscle tissue had to be affected as well. A break was entirely possible, too.

Lucky swore an impressive string of vindictives.

Kneeling beside the horse, he probed the wound. When the horse didn't react too strongly, Pam sensed there was hope the animal's leg wasn't broken. But without an X ray, it would be impossible to tell for sure.

"Get the vet out here, Rafael. On the double." Standing, Lucky soothed his hand over the horse's nose as though he were reassuring his beloved child, then linked his fingers through the bridle. "It's okay, girl. Let's get you back up to the barn."

By now Angie was sitting up. Pam brushed a few bits of grass and dirt from her hair. The child seemed to have survived the accident in better condition than the horse. Even the scrape on her elbow needed no more than a washing with soap and water.

"I'm real, *real* sorry, Lucky," Angie said, her voice filling with a sob. "I was just gonna ride around a little bit—"

"Sorry isn't good enough, Angie."

A muscle ticked at Lucky's jaw, and Pam could hardly blame him for his anger and frustration. Angie had pulled a good many stunts since she'd arrived. But riding Sweet Sigh had been the most dangerous and foolhardy. And the most potentially costly. Even without a break, the deep wound could well take months for the horse to heal enough to race again. Angie's thoughtless antic might have been at the expense of a Kentucky Derby winner—Lucky's dream.

He led the horse up out of the gully. Sweet Sigh stumbled when she reached the pavement.

As though trying desperately to control his temper— or his despair—Lucky gazed up at the gray sky and took a deep breath. Every part of his body radiated a coiled tension that was about to explode. "If Dr. Pam says you're okay, Angie, I want you to go up to your room and stay there. I'll talk to you later."

Angie lowered her head and stared glumly at the ground. "I didn't mean to be bad," she whispered. Her chin quivered. "Just once, before Christmas came, I wanted to ride a horse in case..."

"I believe my grandson is partly to blame," Rafael said.

José, who'd been hanging around the fringes of the accident scene protested. "I tried to stop her, Grandpa. I told her the other day she should stay off Sweet Sigh. She wouldn't listen to me."

"Perhaps you did not try hard enough." The old man gestured up the hill toward the house, fully as angry and upset as Lucky. "Go now. We will discuss your part in this once we have seen to the animal."

Scowling, José jammed his hands in his pockets and stomped away. "I didn't do nothin'," he muttered. "How come I get blamed all the time?"

As Pam watched, Lucky led the limping horse along the roadway. He looked as if he'd just lost his best friend—or his last dollar.

Meanwhile, tears were oozing out of the corners of Angie's eyes. "He's real mad, isn't he?" she asked.

"Yes, I think he is about as angry as a man can be." Pam suspected only some deep well of self-control had prevented Lucky from a far more dramatic display of anger. That he could keep himself so carefully in check was both amazing and admirable.

About then, the wail of a siren announced the arrival of the paramedics, followed closely by a squad car. Pam did her best to explain the situation. Names and addresses were exchanged with the driver of the car, but there seemed little doubt that the blame was Angie's, not his. Fortunately, the car appeared to have survived almost unscathed.

With an admonition to behave herself, Pam sent Angie to her room, promising she'd come up later to clean the child's elbow scrape. Though she certainly lacked veterinary medicine skills, Pam thought she might be able to offer some comfort to Lucky about the well-being of his horse.

She found him in the horse barn gently stroking Sweet Sigh and keeping her calm as Rafael wrapped gauze around the horse's leg. The animal lifted her head and snorted at Pam's arrival.

Glancing up, his eyes bleak, Lucky asked, "How's Angie?"

"Shaken but physically sound except for a few possible bruises. I made sure she went to her room." Pam peered into the stall. "Can I help with Sweet Sigh?"

He shook his head. "The vet's on his way."

"Does he have a portable X-ray machine?"

"Yeah. He's a top-notch guy."

"What happens if..." She had trouble even forming the question.

"The best horse I've ever owned is in pain. I can't begin to think beyond that." He leaned his forehead against Sweet Sigh, wrapping his arms around her elegant neck, his own pain a palpable echo of the injured animal's suffering. "What the hell made Angie do that? She should have known better. God, anybody should have known better."

"Children are unpredictable. Certainly they're impulsive. I know she didn't set off to hurt Sweet Sigh." She shrugged, for in truth, she couldn't explain Angie's behavior either. She simply knew the man she loved, and the child she cared about fiercely, were both in agony. There was nothing in her medical kit that could repair the damage done between them. Somehow they'd have to heal the rift themselves.

IT HAD BEEN HOURS and hours since the accident. Angie had stayed in her room as long as she could. She'd been so scared about what she'd done, she hadn't even had the nerve to talk to Mister Saint Peter. She was sure he'd tell her she'd have come back to heaven because she'd messed up so bad.

She wouldn't blame him. Or Lucky. She'd done a terrible thing.

Peering out into the hallway, nothing but silence greeted her.

She hugged her teddy bear tight up against her chest and took a tentative step forward. Going downstairs wouldn't be a good idea. She might get caught. Then Lucky would be even more mad that she'd disobeyed him than he already was.

Sighing, she wandered down the hallway. The open door to Dr. Pam's bedroom tempted her. She'd only been inside the room a couple of times. She thought she might have another look, only because she knew she'd be close enough to her own room to race back there if she heard Lucky coming into the house.

The bed didn't look like it had been slept in but Dr. Pam was real fussy about making her bed every morning. She'd wanted Angie to make hers, too, but since she was a little kid she couldn't do it as good as a grown-up could. Dr. Pam didn't seem to mind.

The bathroom that was attached to the bedroom had big mirrors all around the room and pretty tiles the same color as Dr. Pam's bedspread on the walls. There were lots of interesting things on the countertop—lipstick and eye goop, and tiny brushes Angie knew women used to paint up their faces when they wanted to look fancy. She was tempted to try fixing her own face with the makeup and stuff but figured this might not be a good day to risk getting into any more trouble.

She was about to leave when she noticed a long, slender box sitting on the counter next to the toilet.

Her eyes widened. She'd seen that kind of a box before. One of her foster mothers, Arlene, had given herself a test with whatever was in that box. Then she'd announced she was going to have a baby—her *own* baby, not a foster kid. Right after that the social worker had moved Angie to another family, one that wasn't nearly so nice as Arlene and her husband.

Angie wanted to swallow but something was filling her throat so full she couldn't. Her breathing grew shallow, like it used to when she was going to have an asthma attack. Sweat beaded her forehead.

She was going to be sent away. She knew it. Mister Saint Peter had lied to her. She wasn't going to get to choose her own parents like he'd said. Even though she'd broken that darn old fertility doll at Dr. Pam's house—one just like the doll at Arlene's house—Dr. Pam was going to have a baby. She wouldn't want Angie around anymore, not when she had a baby of her own.

And Lucky was already so mad at her, he probably wouldn't ever want her around, either.

The lump that had filled Angie's throat turned into tears that spilled down her cheeks. It wasn't fair! she silently sobbed. Every little kid deserved a mother and father, and she'd never, ever had one of her own. Least ways, not any who wanted her.

She snatched the box from the counter. Because she was madder than she'd ever been in her whole, entire life, she twisted and turned and bent the box until she heard the insides crack. Then she tossed it in the waste-basket and ran from the room.

Tomorrow was Christmas. She wasn't going to be here when Mister Saint Peter came to get her like he said he would if the parents she picked didn't want to keep her.

She'd hide, that's what she'd do. She'd hide so far away Mister Saint Peter would never, ever find her. It didn't matter that nobody had ever wanted her, or ever would. If Pam was gonna have a baby, she'd like the baby best and send Angie away. Just like her foster mom had done.

Tears stung at her eyes and blurred her vision as she ran down the stairs.

Her friend José would help her hide. His mom didn't want him, either. Together they'd show everybody, that's what they'd do.

Shoving out her lower lip, she bet Lucky and Dr. Pam and Rafael would sure be sorry when they found out she and José were gone.

Chapter Thirteen

A chipped knee, surgery required.

That was the veterinarian's verdict after a thorough examination of Sweet Sigh, plus a telling X ray. Pam had marveled at the limitations a vet worked under, including patients who couldn't tell him where it hurt. In that regard, his problems in diagnosis were a little like a pediatrician working with a very young child.

She watched from inside the back of the horse barn as Rafael and Lucky got the horse into the vet's trailer for transportation to his clinic. Sweet Sigh went placidly, unaware that surgery, a significant amount of pain, and a long rehabilitative process would soon follow.

The rain that had earlier been misting was beginning to fall more heavily now as the morning slipped into afternoon, and the clouds blanketed the ridge line. Lucky's hair clung damply to his neck in black strands, and his shirt was soaked through on his back.

When he continued to stand in the rain, even after the veterinarian's van and trailer had driven out of sight, Pam went out to get him.

"You're going to catch a chill," she told him gently.

"I'm okay."

"Sure you are. Doctor's orders, come in out of the rain and find some dry clothes to change into." She hooked her arm through his and urged him back into the shelter of the horse barn. The heavy overcast filtered a somber light down the corridor between the stalls. The animals were quiet, as though they wanted to offer sympathy to an injured friend—Lucky or Sweet Sigh, it was hard to know which one they had in mind. "The vet sounded reasonably optimistic, Lucky. Sweet Sigh will be fine."

"You know how long it will be before she can begin training again, much less actually racing?"

"Months, I'd guess." That would certainly be the case with a human athlete who had a chipped bone.

"At least that long. She may never fully recover."

Pam knew he was agonizing over the animal's pain but she suspected there was an even more complicated problem, one he might not be willing to share. "You'd set your heart on her winning the Derby, hadn't you?"

"Yeah. I guess you can wish too hard for something."

"There'll be other horses. Or maybe other years?"

He shook his head. "I sank a lot of money into that filly, hired the best trainer I could find. Then I tried to play it cagey, holding her back until she was ready and could show her stuff. Now? I'm not even sure her foals will bring much on the open market since she doesn't have a record of many races."

Did that mean he had lost his investment? Pam wondered. A familiar and frightening sense of panic whipped through her. The vagaries of horse racing were well beyond her understanding. For all she knew, the loss of his most valuable horse meant Lucky was facing financial ruin. The rent on all manner of assets might be coming due.

She remembered in painful detail the number of times her father's dreams had been shattered or evaporated into smoke. He'd shrugged off the defeat, only to build up his hopes again, and hers, that next week—or next year—he'd get his lucky break. Pam had hated living with so many emotional peaks and valleys. She'd longed for a constancy that simply wasn't a part of her family's financial picture.

As they walked out of the barn, through the pelting rain, and into the house, Lucky said, "I'm going to go up and change, then I'll talk to Angie."

"What are you going to say?"

"I'm not sure. I know if I'd pulled stunt like that as a kid, I would have been horsewhipped."

She raised her eyebrows. "Fortunately, you don't believe in physical violence."

"No. I think a long, serious talk will be far more effective. She's got to be terrified by now. I remember waiting for Rafael to ball me out for something stupid I'd done was far worse than somebody else taking a cane to me."

"Because you cared about him?"

"He's the closest thing I've ever had to a real father."

She brushed a quick kiss to Lucky's cheek. She wanted to tell him how much she loved him—for all the obstacles he'd overcome, for the man he'd *become*. But now was the wrong time. "I told Angie I'd clean up the abrasion she got on her elbow from her fall this morning. It just needs a little soap and water."

"I'll take care of it."

"How 'bout I make us all some hot chocolate. After your talk with Angie, I imagine you'll both need a pick-me-up."

"Thanks." His half smile was a weak imitation of his usual cocky grin; the typical spark in his eyes had turned to a bleakness she hadn't seen before. He was a man capable of great compassion—for a horse or a human being. She loved him for that, too.

While she waited for Lucky's return, Pam took the time to make some sandwiches for their lunch and set out a bag of potato chips. The water for hot chocolate had just started to boil when the overhead light blinked out.

A power failure. Not an unusual occurrence in rural Meadowbrook, particularly during a rainstorm. The creeks were probably running high through the canyons, too. She hoped she didn't get a call from the hospital that they needed her service. With the road so slick, this would not be a good day for traveling.

Lucky came back to the kitchen. Though still damp, his hair had been combed, and he wore a clean shirt and a fresh pair of jeans.

"I can't find Angie," he said.

"She's not in her room?"

"Nope."

"Well, she knows you're upset with her. This is a big house. She's probably hiding."

"I checked in the spare bedrooms. There's no sign of her. Or Tony, her teddy bear."

She frowned. "The bear you gave her?"

"Yeah." He picked up a bologna sandwich, took a bite and rested his hip on the corner of the table. "You figure she'll come out when she gets hungry?"

"That's what usually happens with children. Why don't we wait awhile and then I'll go looking for her? She's probably under a bed somewhere, or has tucked herself way back in a closet. Kids can be very creative about where they hide." She'd heard moms relate how their children had climbed up on closet shelves and hidden behind hat boxes, or slipped into impossibly small spaces under desks—sometimes getting themselves stuck. Angie would turn up. Pam was sure of it.

But after an hour, with the house still ominously quiet, except for the rain running in solid sheets off the roof, Pam went upstairs. She searched Angie's room thoroughly. With a sense of increasing alarm, she found not only was the child's teddy bear missing, so were her sweatshirt and a raincoat Lucky had bought her.

Her apprehension rose as she quickly checked all the places upstairs she thought a small child could hide— under the beds, the backs of closets, inside the laundry hamper. Growing more desperate by the minute, she checked her own room and bathroom.

Suddenly, her heart froze. Icy fingers of fear sped down her spine.

Crumpled at the bottom of the wastebasket was Pam's unused pregnancy test kit. The image of her broken fertility doll flashed through her mind. Angie had *known* about fertility dolls and what they symbolized. And she hadn't wanted any other children in her life.

"Dear heaven . . ."

Whirling, she raced out of the room and down the stairs. She found Rafael standing in the kitchen talking with Lucky. Rain dripped from the foreman's yellow slicker onto the tile floor. Somehow, he looked older than he had before, his dark eyes tortured, his salt-and-pepper eyebrows slanted downward.

"What's wrong?" she asked.

Turning, Lucky said, "José took one of the horses and ran away. He left Rafael a note."

Pam's hand flew to her mouth.

"I think he has gone to see his mother," Rafael explained. "He has never accepted that she does not want him."

Lucky met Pam's gaze. "Any sign of Angie?"

She fought the tightness in her chest. "I think she's run away, too. Dear God, they're probably together." Which was a small blessing. José would know a little about how to survive on his own and would be protective of Angie. But the two of them alone, out there in all this rain? They'd both catch their deaths if they weren't found soon. And Angie had a history of both asthma and pneumonia. A potentially fatal combination if dampness settled into her lungs.

Swearing, Lucky tunneled his fingers through his hair. "It's my fault! I shouldn't have yelled at her. She's just a kid."

"You are not to blame, *hijo*," Rafael insisted. "I was the one who accused my grandson of sharing the responsibility for Sweet Sigh's injury. If I had not been so pigheaded—"

"You're both wrong." Struggling against a sick feeling of dread, Pam clutched the crumpled pregnancy test box in her hand. "If there's any blame to be passed out, I should be on the receiving end. I haven't been entirely honest with you, Lucky."

"About what?"

Silently, she handed him the box. This was hardly the ideal time to announce her pregnancy, or the ideal way. Angie and José were missing, Rafael was right there in the room and there would be no way she and Lucky could discuss their personal relationship. Not now. Finding the children had to be their first priority. But she wanted Lucky to know he wasn't the one who had driven Angie away. She was.

Lucky studied box for a moment, then raised his gaze. "I don't understand."

She drew a steadying breath. "I haven't taken the test yet—largely because I was chicken—but I have a pretty good idea the result would be positive. I think when Angie picked us to be her parents, she had in mind she'd be an only child."

Slowly, the blank look in Lucky's eyes turned to understanding. The corners of his lips edged up. "Are you serious?"

"Very. If I'd told you—"

Rafael, who had been studiously allowing them some small degree of privacy, said, "Please, *señora*, I must go now and find my grandson. The creeks are running very high, and it is dangerous that he and the girl are all alone. He is not yet that good a rider."

Rafael's warning galvanized Lucky into action. "Pam, you call the police and get us some help to search the entire area. The kids can't have gone far. Not in this weather. Rafael and I will start looking now. We'll probably have them back none the worse for wear by the time the cops get here." Lucky ran the back of his knuckles lightly down her cheek, wiping away a tear she hadn't realized had fallen. "And when we get Angie back home, you and I are going to have a long talk. I promise."

"ARE WE LOST, José?"

"Maybe a little. But you told me to stay off the road so nobody would see us."

"I know." Shivering, Angie put her head down so the rain wouldn't blow in her face. She was sitting in front of José on Hot Diggity, but riding a horse didn't seem like that much fun anymore. It was almost dark and she was cold, real cold.

"Maybe we should go back," José said glumly.

Clutching her teddy bear under her raincoat, Angie knew she couldn't go back. Everybody was real mad at her 'cause she'd messed up so bad, and Saint Peter was gonna come get her. "Don't you still want to see your mom?"

"Sure. But maybe we could pick another day. Like when it's sunny, or somethin'. It keeps raining harder and harder. I can't even see where we're going."

Just then the horse slipped on wet rock and stumbled. Angie hung on tight to his dark mane. They were walking along a creek bank hoping to figure out a way to cross the stream but the water was churning so loud and fast, they couldn't find any shallow place that looked safe enough to try.

"Man, this is the pits! We're gonna get ourselves killed." José reined the horse around. "I don't care what you say, I'm going back."

Angie tightened her jaw stubbornly. She had a lot more to lose than José. He, at least, had a grandpa. She didn't have nobody. "I bet you don't even know how to get home," she challenged.

"I do so!"

The horse slipped again, sinking into the rain-loosened soil along the edge of the flooded creek. Angie pitched forward. She tried to hang on. But her fingers slipped and she slid off to one side.

"José!"

"Geez, Angie—"

She splashed into the muddy water. More of the bank gave way beneath the horse's weight, tumbling dirt and debris into the stream. Fighting her way to her feet, coughing and spitting, Angie staggered sideways.

A wall of water slammed into her, knocking her down again. She swallowed another mouthful of water. The current wrenched her toward the middle of the creek. Flailing her arms, she tried to swim. But she'd never learned how. Foster kids didn't have much chance to take lessons.

She couldn't catch her breath. It was dark and cold and wet, and her arms felt like she'd turned into a Raggedy Ann doll. She bounced off one rock and then another.

"José!" she screamed when her head popped above the surface of the water. Then the current dragged her under again, the darkness growing deeper and blacker until she didn't feel so cold anymore. The stream pulled and tugged at her, tossing her from side to side. She felt like she was floating now, the same feeling she'd had the night her house had burned down in North Dakota and her chest had filled with smoke. It didn't really hurt too much, until her head hit a rock hidden under the water.

Limp, she stopped fighting the current. She guessed Mister Saint Peter was gonna have to write her name in his book after all.

LUCKY CHAFED AT Chief Coleman's instructions to get back home and stay put. "We don't want a bunch of civilians out here getting lost or worse," he had said when he found Lucky out in the rain searching for Angie on his own. "We'll find the youngsters faster if we don't have to worry about you or the doctor doing something foolish."

So he'd gone home and paced the floors with Pam, waiting for the phone to ring or Angie to show up in a police car. The house was so damn quiet, Lucky knew he and Pam had to fill that silence. The subject most on his mind—outside of finding Angie—was the baby. *His* baby.

He speared his fingers through his hair. "How 'bout we talk a little . . . about, you know . . ."

She glanced at him from across the living room. Her eyes were red rimmed, her movements radiating tension. "I feel like such a fool, Lucky. I'm a doctor. Of all people, I should have insisted we take precautions. I simply wasn't thinking."

Lucky didn't know quite how to respond. He only knew he was scared. Real scared—for Angie, who was still missing long after dark, and because he wanted Pam and their baby more than anything he could ever remember wanting in his whole life. Except he wanted Angie, too, and everything had gotten into a huge muddle.

"Why weren't you thinking?" he asked cautiously. Though Lucky realized he hadn't exactly been responsible himself. It definitely took two to make a baby. He wondered why *with Pam,* and no other woman in the past, he had totally forgotten that elemental truth.

Arms folded, she stared out the picture window into the dark night where the rain was still falling. They hadn't turned on the Christmas lights and the colorfully wrapped presents looked forlorn under the dark tree. He remembered a more joyous time, an evening when she had shared herself without hesitation, there beneath the tree.

"I didn't think I could get pregnant. Ted and I had tried for three years. I wanted babies . . ." Her voice caught. "He told me it was my fault."

Lucky swallowed back a few choice words to describe Pam's deceased husband. "He was wrong."

"Worse. He lied. When I began to suspect that we . . . you and I . . . I checked with his doctor. Ted was the one who couldn't have children. He'd told the doctor the clinic was his 'baby' and that we both thought 'giving birth' to the clinic was enough. He was wrong, so terribly wrong. In fact, I've already arranged to sell the clinic as soon as I can. I want to be able to spend more time with the baby." In a telling gesture, her hand slid across her midsection.

At the sound of her sob, Lucky closed the distance between them. He wrapped his arms around her. "It's okay, sweetheart. Everything's going to be okay." My God, she was giving up her dream—the clinic she'd worked so hard to make a success—to take care of *his* baby. He wanted to jump for joy.

"You don't have to marry me, you know. This is the nineties. I mean, women have babies all the time and they don't have to... Without taking the pregnancy test, I'm not even a hundred percent sure—"

"I am." He was sure he wanted to marry Pam and wanted her to have his babies—lots of them. But he wasn't all that confident she reciprocated his feelings. From the beginning, she'd been stubbornly resistant to their relationship. Now she didn't want to marry him even though she was carry his baby. What did a man have to do to convince this woman their marriage had been arranged in heaven?

The ringing phone jarred the silence between them.

Pam was closest and got there first. Her expression tightened as she listened to the caller. Her chin trembled; a sheen of tears sprang to her eyes.

Without responding to the person on the other end of the line, she replaced the telephone in its cradle. "They've found Angie."

Chapter Fourteen

"I messed up, didn't I?"

"It would seem you made some serious errors in judgment," Saint Peter agreed. He looked a little tired tonight, like he'd been real busy. Maybe he was like Santa Claus and had to work extra hard on Christmas Eve. 'Cept Angie never had much believed in Santa.

"I got too greedy. I know that now. There are things lots more important than having a horse." Like having a mom and dad and a nice warm bed to sleep in.

"It is well when we can learn from our mistakes."

She sighed, feeling defeated. "Guess you'll have to write my name in your big book after all."

"Why would you wish me to do that?"

"'Cause you said I had to find parents who wanted me before Christmas or I'd have to come back up here." She lifted her shoulders in a dejected shrug. "Here I am.'

With an indulgent smile, he brushed her damp bangs back from her forehead. "So you believe you have failed in your quest for parents of your very own?"

"I tried real hard but I wasn't good enough. Lucky's so mad he probably doesn't ever want to see me again. And Dr. Pam is gonna have her own baby, so she doesn't need me to be her little girl." She sniffed back a tear. "I thought you were gonna help me, Mister Saint Peter. You promised."

"Perhaps you have jumped to a hasty conclusion. The baby that is growing in Pamela's womb is a boy. She still might want to have a daughter, an older child who could teach the baby all the things that are important on earth—and in heaven."

"You think so?"

"I do." He adjusted the way he was holding her on his lap, letting her rest her head on his shoulder. "It seems to me Lucky has expressed considerable fondness for you. You might want to give him another chance to be a father."

"I should?"

"If there were parents somewhere in the world who loved you very much, and thought you had drowned in that creek, what do you imagine they would be doing now?"

She furrowed up her forehead. Nobody had ever loved her, least ways, none that she knew about. "I guess maybe they'd be crying."

"Why don't you take a look and see what Lucky and Pamela are doing?"

Squirming sideways, she peered over the edge of the clouds. She saw herself in a hospital bed with all kinds of wires and stuff stuck in her and a big bandage wrapped around her head. It looked like she was asleep and might never wake up again.

Dr. Pam and Lucky were standing beside her, and they both looked super sad. There were big teardrops rolling down Dr. Pam's cheeks. Lucky had his arm around the doctor's shoulders and his eyes were kinda red and puffy, like he'd been crying, too. Angie had never, ever seen a grown-up man cry. It didn't make Lucky look sissy at all. In fact, it made him look like a daddy who was super-duper special.

"Are they crying because of me?" she asked.

"Yes. They both love you very much, Angelica. By running away you made them quite unhappy."

"I didn't mean to make them feel bad. I wish I could go back and fix it so they wouldn't be sad anymore. But it's too late, isn't it?"

"Not yet. It is still several minutes until midnight and the time when all of God's littlest angels need to be here in heaven to help celebrate Christmas."

Her eyes widened. "You mean I can go back?"

He smiled. "Of course, Angelica. I gave you my promise, didn't I?"

"Oh, wow!" She hopped down off his lap. "I'll be real good this time. And I won't be greedy. I double, *double* promise I won't be."

"You'd better hurry, Angelica. Your time is almost up."

She started to leave, then cocked her head. "Mister Saint Peter, if I mess up again . . . I mean, if I need your help to fix somethin', will you still be around?"

He nodded solemnly. "All you need to do is call me, and I'll be there."

"Thanks, Mister Saint Peter. I'll remember that. 'Cause sometimes it's real hard for us little kids to be good all the time. I might need you again someday."

EVEN THOUGH LUCKY held her tight, Pam couldn't stop trembling. She was a trained physician but she'd lost all semblance of objectivity. She simply wanted Angie to live. "She looks so tiny," she whispered. Pursing her lips, she tried to halt the sob that threatened.

"We're lucky José got help as fast as he did after she fell in the creek. Otherwise..." His voice caught as though he couldn't bear to finish the thought.

"Lucky, I love her so much. I don't want to lose her."

"She'll make it. I'd lay odds on it."

"Comas can last for days or weeks. The body weakens—"

"She's a pretty tough cookie. Like you, sweetheart. She'll be fine."

"But that doesn't mean... You wanted to be her daddy from the beginning. I was sort of an add-on so the authorities would let you keep her."

"Is that what you think?" He rubbed his cheek against the side of her head. "I'm a proud man, Pam, but I'm not above groveling when I need to. I know you're scared to death you'll end up with some guy like your brother-in-law. Or your father."

"I love my father," she objected. "It's just—"

"If you're afraid I'm broke, don't be. My financial situation has probably taken a pretty big hit with Sweet Sigh's injury, but I've still got some decent horses left."

"Your money isn't important to me. Or what you do for a living. If it was once and I was guilty of being a small-town snob, that's not true anymore."

"You're sure?"

"Positive." She'd be happy living with Lucky in a barn, if that was all they could afford. Suddenly she wondered if her mother had felt the same way about her father and knew in her heart of hearts that had to be true. How odd she hadn't realized that before, that the importance of love made everything else pale by comparison.

"If you want, I'll sell my horses and get a nine-to-five job."

"You'd be miserable. Why would you want to do that?"

"Because I don't want to lose you any more than either of us want to lose Angie."

At the sound of her name, Angie groaned.

"She's coming around," Pam said, leaning forward. "Come on, little munchkin. Open your eyes. It's almost time for Christmas. You don't want to miss that."

Slowly, Angie's eyelids fluttered opened. She focused and a tiny smile played at the corners of her lips. "Hi."

Relief swept through Pam so swiftly she couldn't manage to speak.

"Hi, yourself, sport." Lucky took the child's hand.

"I'm real sorry I hurt Sweet Sigh."

"I know you are. She's going to be all right. She's in a hospital right now, just like you. The vet's gonna fix her up."

"I'm glad."

"What we need to have happen here is for you to get well, too. See, there's a little mare just waiting to belong to a very special little girl like you."

Angie's eyes widened to full wakefulness. "A horse? Of my very own?"

"You bet, sport. I figure that's the one present you wanted most of all for Christmas. So it's yours. As soon as the doctor lets you out of the hospital."

Slowly, she shook her head. "That's not the one present I really and truly wanted more than anything else in the whole wide world."

"It's not?"

Pam stroked Angie's soft cheek with her fingertips. "Then what was it you wanted, honey?"

Her young eyes filled with tears. "A mommy and daddy of my very own. If I could have that, then Lucky could give the horse to some other little girl who didn't have anybody to love."

Emotion tightened a band around Pam's chest.

Lucky cleared his throat as though he were fighting the same strong feelings Pam was experiencing. "I love you, sport. More than you'll ever know."

"Just like you love Dr. Pam?"

His gaze met Pam's with such intensity, her breath caught and her heart did a wild somersault as if she were on a roller coaster.

"I love the doc in a different way," he said softly, his agate blue eyes filled with the love he was proclaiming. "A way so special, only a guy like Shakespeare could explain it. Not somebody like me who never graduated from high school. I wouldn't be able to find all the words I'd need."

"Does that mean you and Dr. Pam are going to get married?" Angie asked.

"If she's fool enough to have me." He reached in his pocket and pulled out a small box, flipping open the lid to reveal a huge diamond ring.

Pam drew a quick breath. "When did you get that?"

"A couple of days ago. I was planning to give it to you tonight, right on the stroke of midnight."

"You bought it before you knew...before I told you I was..."

"That's right. Whether you're pregnant or not doesn't matter. I want you to be my wife." He glanced up at the wall clock where the minute hand ticked toward the twelve.

"Please say yes, Dr. Pam," Angie urged. "Before it's midnight. I promise I'll be a real good big sister for your little baby boy. I'll teach him lots of good stuff. Honest, I will."

Pam slid a surprised gaze toward Angie. "A boy?"

Angie smiled smugly. "Mister Saint Peter said so."

"Oh, my..." Things were moving too fast for Pam, leaving her feeling thoroughly unsettled. Desperately, she tried to keep her feet solidly planted in reality. "About the ring, Lucky. It's so big. Far too extravagant. It must be three or four carats."

"Three and a half. I couldn't find anything bigger on such short notice."

"But the expense! You've got the veterinarian bill to pay for Sweet Sigh. We'll have the baby to think about and Angie, too. We've got to start thinking about her schooling—"

"Will you stop being so darn practical, Doc," he said, laughing. "This is the ring I want you to have— assuming you like it, of course."

"It's gorgeous. What woman wouldn't want it? But it must have cost—"

"Think of it as your insurance policy against being broke, if you'd like. You can always pawn it."

She glared at him, her jaw tightening. "I'd rather starve first." Taking the ring from the box, she held it between her fingers. The overhead lights caught the facets and cast them in a thousand brilliant colors, a miracle of rainbows. "You'd better mean this, O'Toole. Because once I make up my mind, I'm not a quitter. It'll be darn hard to get rid of me."

"I figure, with Angie's help, our marriage has been made in heaven. It'll last a lifetime. Maybe longer."

Angie tugged on his sleeve. "Does that mean I gets to be your little girl?"

"I can't wait till I get to go to father-daughter teas, or whatever they have these days. I'll be the proudest papa around."

"Oh, Angie, of course you'll be our little girl. I already feel like I'm your mother."

Lucky lifted Pam's chin. His eyes sparkled. "Did you just say yes to my proposal?"

"I certainly did. Don't you know how much I love you, Lucky?"

A big grin creased his cheeks. "That's great. Really great."

"Then would you mind telling me you love me, too?"

He looked nonplussed. "Didn't I say that?"

"Not to me, you didn't. You told Angie. I want to hear it again to be sure you really mean it."

"How 'bout I show you instead?"

"That won't do, O'Toole. I want to hear the words." She realized he'd had few people in his life whom he had felt free to love. She wanted to be among the very first. Along with Angie, of course.

His big hands gently framed Pam's face. "I love you, Pamela Jones. I love the baby that's growing inside your belly, and I want to marry you. I want us to be a family—the four of us, including Angie. And maybe there will be more babies later on 'cause they would have such a terrific, levelheaded mom." Dipping his head, he crossed her lips with a kiss that confirmed his promise, deep and hot and compelling.

Sweet warmth stole through Pam's limbs and she sighed. "You're a very persuasive man, O'Toole."

"You got that right, sweetheart."

Outside, the church bells in town began striking the hour, welcoming Christmas.

Angie smiled up at the ceiling above her bed, squares filled with holes that made it look like a giant speaker for a stereo set. She winked. "Thanks, Mister Saint Peter."

You're welcome, Angelica. Have a very merry Christmas.

A HOLIDAY RECIPE FROM THE KITCHEN OF

Charlotte Maclay

This is a perfect light supper for Christmas Eve—or to serve a couple of days after the holiday when the family has tired of leftovers. The first time I tried this recipe I didn't have all the right ingredients, so I improvised. Thus "Mistake" became a family favorite that I've passed on to my daughters. Let me know if you enjoy it, too: P.O. Box 505, Torrance, CA 90508

ENCHILADA MISTAKE

1 lb ground meat
1 can chile con carne
1 onion, diced
1 package refrigerator biscuits
1/2 cup cornmeal
1 cup shredded sharp cheddar cheese
black olives (optional)

Brown meat in a heavy skillet; drain excess fat. Add chile and half of onion. Cover and cook over medium heat for 10 minutes. Meanwhile, using waxed paper, roll 4 biscuits in cornmeal until they are flat like a tortilla. Lightly brown on a griddle. In a baking pan make two stacks by layering biscuit/tortilla, meat mixture, cheese, remaining onion and olives. Bake at 350° F for 20 minutes, or until heated through. Serves 4.
(Remaining biscuits may be baked and served with the meal.)

You asked for it...You got it! More MEN!

We're thrilled to bring you another special edition of the popular MORE THAN MEN series.

Like those who have come before him, Adam Walsh is more than tall, dark and handsome. All of those men have extraordinary powers that make them "more than men." But whether they are able to grant you three wishes, or live forever, make no mistake—their greatest, most extraordinary power is of seduction.

So make a date with Adam Walsh in...

#663 ADAM'S KISS
by Mindy Neff
January 1997

203

What's a woman to do when she hasn't got a date for New Year's Eve? *Buy* a man, that's what!

And make sure it's one of the eligible

That's exactly what friends Dana Shaw and Elise Allen do in the hilarious New Year's Bachelors duet. But the men they get give these women even more than they bargained for!

Don't miss:

#662 DANA & THE CALENDAR MAN
by Lisa Bingham
January 1997

#666 ELISE & THE HOTSHOT LAWYER
by Emily Dalton
February 1997

Ring in the New Year with NEW YEAR'S BACHELORS!